Eye
of the
Alpha

Sharee Hidalgo

Fulton Books
Meadville, PA

Published by Fulton Books 2022

ISBN 978-1-63710-883-3 (paperback)
ISBN 978-1-63710-884-0 (digital)

Printed in the United States of America

This book is dedicated to mi patrón, Juan Francisco Melchor Serrano, who COVID-19 stole away from us. You were the first person to read my story and encourage me to get it published. *Descansa en paz.*

Chapter 1

"Gabriela! Hurry up! This stuff better be cleared off the floor before I get back."

Gabriela let out a silent sigh as she heard her uncle screaming from downstairs. She rushed downstairs, not wanting to make him upset again.

"Put them upstairs in the hall. I will help you sort them," said her aunt.

Gabriela only nodded in response. She chose not to verbally answer out of anger and fear. Gabriela resented her aunt and uncle because of how they treated her…her uncle more than her aunt.

"Gabi…please don't shut me out," she pleaded. "I know you're hurt and you're upset. You have every right to be but we can't—"

"Please… I want to get this done before he gets back. You're not the one he takes his anger out on." Gabriela grabbed a box off the floor as her aunt grabbed her arm.

"I promise it won't be like this forever. He's going to change."

Gabriela rolled her eyes as she headed back toward the steps with the box. It hurt her that her own mother's sister allowed her husband to beat her whenever he pleased while she just watched. Her aunt had promised her mother before she died that she would look after her on her deathbed. Her mother died when she was five, forcing her to be sent to live with her aunt and uncle, but the beatings didn't start until she turned eleven. She shuddered as she heard the front door open again.

"Gabriela!"

"Coming!" She rushed back down the steps. Once in the landing, she approached him cautiously. "Yes, sir?"

"You're starting school tomorrow." He stalked toward her, causing her to shrink back in fear. "You will not make a scene here. Do you understand? If we have to move again, I will break your ankles!"

Gabriela lowered her gaze to ground as she nodded her head. He blamed her for them having to move again because the last time he beat her before she went to school, she didn't do a well enough job to hide the cuts and bruises. She flinched as he let out a growl of frustration.

"Use your words!" he yelled as he grabbed her arms forcefully. "If I have to pack up one more time, you won't be able to walk when I'm done with you!" He pushed her to the ground and began to kick her in the stomach and ribs repeatedly.

"Yes! I understand," she cried out between blows. She cried out once more as he delivered a final kick to her ribs before retreating to the kitchen.

"Why didn't you speak up sooner?" said her aunt, dropping to her knees to try to comfort her.

"Please…leave me alone," she sobbed. She didn't want to be anywhere near them. Her uncle beats her while her aunt keeps quiet until he leaves the room. It disgusted her. She laid on the floor for a few more moments before she struggled to stand.

Gabriela hissed in pain with each step that she took as she climbed the stairs. She made her way to the bathroom and turned on the shower. She knew that she wouldn't get to eat tonight with her uncle's foul mood. She stood under the water, allowing it to mix with the silent tears that fell from her eyes. Once she finished her shower, she carefully got dressed and quietly snuck into her room.

"What…too good to have dinner with your family?" Her uncle's voice startled her.

"No sir… I—"

"Shut up! Did I say you could get up off the floor?" He grinned at her. "Come here."

Gabriela padded across the room toward her uncle as she unsuccessfully tried to hold back the tears that fell down her cheeks. She knew that she was going to be lucky if she could move tomorrow when he was done with her. Without warning, he reached behind her head, yanking her head back by her hair so hard that she lost her balance and stumbled backward to the floor. She instinctively brought her arms down to her stomach to try and protect her already cracked ribs. He began his assault of kicks to her stomach and ribs again, kicking her arms in the process. After what seemed like an eternity, his blows slowed to a stop.

"Don't be late tomorrow and keep your mouth shut!" he hissed as he walked out, slamming the door behind him.

Gabriela tried to lay completely still as she cried on the floor. Her lungs burned, and it hurt to breathe. She tried to raise her right hand to wipe the tears from her face and yelped in pain. She could barely move her arm and couldn't feel her fingers. *I can't take much more of this*, she thought to herself as she drifted off to sleep on the floor.

Chapter 2

Gabriela groaned as she struggled to get off the floor. She looked toward the window and saw that the sun was starting to rise. *I'd rather be early than late to school*, she thought to herself. She also knew that the more time she spent out of the house, the less time she would spend being beaten. She painfully changed her clothes before heading to the bathroom to brush her teeth. Once she was done getting ready, she grabbed her schoolbag before tiptoeing down the stairs. She made her way to the kitchen, grabbing a banana.

"You don't have to sneak around. He left already."

"Thanks," mumbled Gabriela as she turned to leave the kitchen.

"Gabi, please. Listen, I know you are not happy, but you don't understand why he's like this," her aunt pleaded.

"You're really defending him? No excuse you tell me can justify why you let him treat me like a punching bag!" she gritted out. "I can't breathe! I can't move my arm or feel my fingers. He's going to end up killing me…"

"I'm not defending him," she protested.

"But you're not defending me either." Gabriela let out a painful sigh. "It doesn't matter. It never does… I gotta go. I don't want to be late to school." She walked out of the kitchen, leaving her aunt calling behind her. She couldn't listen to her aunt try to beg for forgiveness yet again. She held the paper with her left hand that had the school's information. She had no idea where the school was or how to get there. Right as she went to walk down the walkway, her uncle's car pulled up.

"Get in the car," he called out to her.

She made her way down to the car and slid into the passenger seat.

"Good choice of clothes." He studied the long jeans and long-sleeved shirt. "Pay attention to how to get there because you're going to be walking."

"Yes sir," she responded quietly as she looked out of the passenger window.

After a ten-minute drive, her uncle pulled into the school parking lot. "Go to the office and get your schedule. Tell them you don't need a bus."

"Yes sir," she responded softly once more as she used her left hand to open the door. She quickly walked around the vehicle to make her way to the building but yelped when her uncle got out of the car and grabbed her right arm.

"Remember my warning," he growled, gripping her arm tighter.

Gabriela nodded as she tried to blink back her ears. When he yanked her arm again, she cried out, "Yes, sir!" She sobbed. "I remember!"

Gabriela and her uncle were so caught up in her pain that they didn't notice the group of boys approaching them.

"Hey!" yelled one of them as they approached the car. "Is something wrong?"

"No, just talking with my niece." He gripped her harm harder as he twisted it a little, sending her a silent warning to keep her mouth shut. "Isn't that right, Gabi?"

Not trusting the tone in her voice to betray her, she simply nodded as she stared at the ground. Her uncle released her arm, nodding his head at her, motioning for her to head into the school.

"What warning was she supposed to remember?" asked the same boy from earlier.

Gabriela froze at his question. How did he hear her uncle when he was nowhere near the car? Not sure on what she should do, she glanced at her uncle who was already seething with anger.

"I don't know what you're talking about. Gabi, get to class," he ordered. "I changed my mind. I will be picking you up from school today."

She simply nodded as she turned to head toward the school. She knew that the longer her uncle stayed out there with those boys, the more questions they would ask. Making her way through the two sets of double doors, she made her way to the office to collect her class schedule along with her locker details. She followed the poorly printed map to her locker and began to work on the combination. *This would be a whole lot easier if I could use my right hand,* she thought to herself. She tried two more times unsuccessfully before leaning her head against the locker in frustration.

"Having trouble?"

She slowly turned around to see the same group of boys from earlier. She simply shook her head before turning around to try the combination one more time.

"How about I help you?" he offered as he held his hand out.

She handed him the paper with the combination as she looked at the ground.

"Hey, I know we're scary looking, but you don't have to look at the floor," he joked as he opened the locker.

She nodded as she slid past him to awkwardly start putting things in her locker. Her cheeks burned as she could feel the group of boys watching her from behind.

"What's your name?" he asked. He waited a few seconds before offering his, "I'm Seth." When she didn't respond, he took a step closer to her. "If you don't want to tell me your name, that's cool."

He observed her as she struggled with one hand trying to get herself situated to start the day. "Here, let me help you," he offered as he reached for her right arm.

Letting out a painful hiss, she dropped her books as he touched her arm. This was exactly what wasn't supposed to happen today. No attention. Those were his exact words. She kneeled down to try and grab her books again with one hand.

"Stop," commanded Seth. "Let me help you," he said in a softer tone as he reached for her books this time. "What's your first class?" he asked.

When she didn't reply again, he let out a growl, causing Gabriela to flinch away from him. He silently gathered her books and grabbed her schedule. She obviously was afraid to interact with him. "Looks like we have all the same classes. Here. Follow me," he said softly as he touched her right arm again without thinking, causing her to hiss in pain.

Seth stopped dead in his tracks at her reaction. He tried to excuse the first noise she made when he touched her as her being shy and not liking to be touched, but this time, it was undeniable. She was hurt.

Seth

"Man, I wish my father would just stop setting up all these pack meets," groaned Seth. His father was the alpha werewolf of the Black Paw Pack. "He expects me to get good grades, learn pack stuff, and find a mate!"

"If you would stop getting in trouble, he'd lay off," said Jace. Jace was his beta and his best friend. "That way, we'd stop getting in trouble too," he laughed.

"No one told you guys to follow me. We all know I always get caught." He grinned. "Early pack duties at the school though? That's torture!"

The group of werewolves made their way through the wall of trees nearing their high school, stepping through the last row of trees near the parking lot.

"Who's that?" questioned Jace, motioning to a newer model sedan parked at the school.

Seth and the others watched the man grab the girl, causing her to cry out in pain.

"Remember my warning," they heard him growl as he gripped her arm tightly.

"Someone who needs to learn to keep his hands to himself," growled Seth as they approached the car.

"Hey!" yelled Seth as they approached the car.

"Is something wrong?" Seth led his group of wolves up to the car when he caught the scent of the girl before him. His wolf stirred within, causing his eyes to glow. She was his mate. His excitement immediately disappeared when he saw how tight the man's grip was on his mate's arm.

"No, just talking with my niece." The man gripped her harm harder as he twisted, causing him to let out a feral growl as he continued to silently threaten his mate. "Isn't that right, Gabi?" he snickered.

Seth watched the man tell her he'd pick her up for school before watching his mate scurry toward the school. Once she was safely within the school, he cleared his throat. "Sir… I'm going to assume your new here…but let me make myself clear, keep your hands to yourself," he growled.

"Mind your own business, boy." The man glared at Seth and the others. "And keep away from my niece."

"What an ass," Jace said as they watched the car peel out of the parking lot. "That chick is gonna have a bruise from his grip."

Seth let out another feral growl at his comment; this one noticeably louder than the last.

"Seth, what's your problem? You sound like a territorial chihuahua."

"Him!" he growled. "He had his hands on my mate!"

Chapter 3

Seth escorted Gabriela to the first class that they had together. He tried to get her to open up and talk to him, but he could tell how afraid she was. He wasn't sure if it was because she was shy on her first day or because of the asshole that dropped her off this morning. Once in class, he made sure to sit directly behind her. He could tell that she was uncomfortable with his presence, but he didn't want to be away from her. He mind-linked his beta to sit next to her. He wasn't particularly fond of allowing another male to be near his mate, but he needed someone he could trust to look after her.

Seth, I think something is wrong with your mate... mind-linked Jace.

What do you mean? he responded through the link.

Her arm...she keeps rubbing it like it hurts, and it looks like she's struggling to take notes with her other hand.

Seth's wolf stirred with anger, letting out a low growl. He noticed Gabriela's body stiffen at the sound, along with the other students in the room.

The teacher shot him a look before sending him a message through the mind link. *Seth, how many times do I have to tell you to control yourself! There are humans in this class!*

Knowing that the teacher would report directly back to his father, he responded through the link. *I'm sorry,* he began. *The human in front of me is my mate. She needs to see the nurse.* Seth closed the link as the teacher nodded at him and began to speak again.

"Class, we are going to do an exercise. Since we have a new student in class, we are all going to learn something new about each other." He leaned against his desk before speaking again. "I am going to make a statement...raise your right hand for yes...and left hand for no."

Seth studied his mate's body language as the teacher began. "Raise your hand if you're an only child," the teacher said. Hands went up everywhere around the class...except one. Hers. "I don't see everyone's hands up," announced the teacher. The teacher gave Seth an apologetic look before continuing.

"Excuse me, can I use the bathroom?" asked Gabriela. She rushed from the room with Seth close behind.

"Hey! Wait...," he called out to her. "Please!" he pleaded with her as he chased her down the hall. Without thinking, he reached out for her injured arm and regretted it instantly when she cried out in pain. "I'm sorry... I didn't mean to hurt you." He held his hands up in surrender to show her he meant no harm.

"Please, go away...just leave me alone," she pleaded.

"I just want to help. I know your arm is hurt." He took a step toward her as she took a step back from him. "I can walk you to the nurse," he offered.

She shook her head. "It's fine. I'm fine," she protested.

"Then raise your right arm," he ordered.

When she averted her gaze from his eyes to the floor, he knew that she couldn't protest.

"That's what I thought. Now, follow me to the nurse." He guided her gently by her left arm down the hall to the nurse's office. He smiled to himself as he inhaled her scent, completely oblivious to the school slut positioned at the end of the hall.

"Hi, Seth," purred Jessica. "I've been waiting here for you for over an hour."

Seth rolled his eyes. He had forgotten all about their plan to ditch school. "Yeah, I was busy," he responded, passing her by without so much as a glance back. He knew that she was only interested in him because he was the alpha's son, and she wanted to be his luna. He never minded her advances toward him, but now he felt disgusted by the mere sound of her voice.

"It's okay. I can walk with you, and we can go once you're done with…her." Her tone was unmistakably belittling toward Gabriela.

"Don't bother, Jessica, I will be busy…with her." He smirked as he continued to walk. He felt his wolf itching to let out a warning growl but had to suppress it, not wanting to scare his mate. After leaving Jessica huffing and pouting in the hallway, they finally made it to the nurse's office.

"Young Al—" started the nurse but froze when she saw Seth shaking his head for her not to continue her sentence. "Seth…how can I help you?" She was the pack doctor and school nurse. She gave Gabriela a warm smile as she approached them.

"Um…my class*mate* needs to be seen." He added a certain tone to the "mate" part of classmate, hoping that the nurse caught on. Seeing the recognition in her response, he nodded with a smile.

"I understand. I can evaluate her. Would you like me to call you when I'm done?" she asked.

He shook his head. "No, I will wait in the hall."

He gave Gabriela a soft smile as he walked out of the room, closing the door behind him. As soon as he closed the door, he pulled out his phone to call his dad. He needed to let him know that he had found his mate but more importantly how he found his mate. He needed answers, and he needed them now.

Gabriela

She watched as Seth closed the door. She was tempted to try and run from him, but he seemed determined to get her to the nurse, which meant another beating when she got home. Feeling the pit of fear grow in her stomach, she took a step back away from the nurse in a panic.

"I shouldn't be here... I'm sorry I wasted your time." She turned toward the door when the nurse reached for her injured arm.

The nurse released her arm as soon as she heard Gabriela unsuccessfully try to stifle a yelp. "It looks to me like you should be here," she said to her. She motioned for her to follow her to the cot and pulled out a sheet of paper to take notes. "I can obviously see you have an injury to your arm...care to explain what happened?"

"I fell." She looked away. She was a horrible liar, which was why she always got caught trying to make up excuses for all the injuries she has received over the years.

"Great, so since you fell... I'm going to take an x-ray of your arm. How high up does it hurt?"

"It's just sore… I don't need an x-ray. I really need to get back to class, Miss…," she started to say when she didn't know the nurses name.

"Kara. I don't make the kids use 'miss.' It makes me feel old," she joked. "Look. I promise if you don't want me to ask questions right now, I won't…but you need to get your arm looked at. Can you please tell me how high up your arm the pain reaches?"

She nodded before responding. "My shoulder."

"Thank you…now let's get yourself looked at."

She led Gabriela into a small room in the back. Not wanting to push her to do too much, she decided to have her lay flat on the x-ray table to get an image of her shoulders down to her waist.

Kara, I'm going crazy out here…how is she doing? Seth asked in through the link.

Not very good, young alpha. How much do you know about your mate?

Not much. That her ass of an uncle talks to her like shit…why?

Kara hesitated before responding. *I think he does more than just talk to her like shit. Her shoulder is dislocated, her arm is fractured along with two fingers, and she has four cracked ribs. I haven't—*Kara didn't get to finish explaining her diagnosis before she heard the door to the office swing open and slam shut.

"What do you mean she—" he yelled before Kara cut him off.

"Please, Seth. You have to wait outside. She's shaken up enough as it is…you being here is going to make convincing her much harder for me."

"What are you talking about?" Seth was becoming agitated that his mate was in such poor physical health for a human.

"You have to remain calm if I tell you." Seth nodded, waiting for her to continue. "She won't let me cast her arm. I need to set and cast it, but she won't do it…something about it is too obvious, and it will show."

Seth's wolf whimpered that his mate wouldn't allow Kara to help her. "Why not just sedate her? If she's sleep, she can't protest."

"I can't just sedate humans, your father would have my head."

"Not if he knew it was for my mate's well-being." Seth grinned at Kara, knowing he was right, but he also knew that she wouldn't do it unless his father was here to give the okay.

Seth chuckled. "He's already on his way here to see her…we can just tell him what's going on. He will be okay with it… I mean he sedated and kidnapped my mother."

"Fine, when he gets here…we will ask him." Kara's reply was skeptical, but she knew that Seth wouldn't take no for an answer.

"Ask me what?" came the Alpha's voice from behind them. "Son, where is she? Where's your mate?"

"That's just it, Dad…we have a problem."

Seth explained the details of his encounter with Gabriela and her uncle while Kara excused herself from the room. She wanted to try to keep convincing the young alpha's mate to allow her to set and treat her arm. "I know that humans are fragile and weird, Dad, but this…something is not right. She's afraid to let Kara treat her because people will see her cast!"

"Calm down. I will allow Kara to sedate her. We will take her home and meet her uncle. If he is as bad as you say he is, we will take care of that if the time comes." Seth's father stood up and brushed the imaginary dust off his shirt. "Now…introduce me to this mate of yours."

Chapter 4

Gabriela's eyes cracked open slowly. She squinted her eyes as she scanned the room, trying to focus her blurry vision.

"Look who's awake," said Seth's soft voice. "How do you feel?"

She focused her eyes in the direction of his voice. "Why do you care?" she asked, struggling to sit up.

Seth rushed over to help her into a sitting position. "Because I do."

"Well, you shouldn't." She slid off the cot to stand but collapsed into Seth's arms, gasping in shock when she reached to put her arms out for balance.

"What is this?" she shrieked in horror. "I said I didn't want a cast!" She held out the pink and purple cast that reached from her forearm down to her ring finger and pinky.

"I know, but you were hurt. Kara didn't have a choice," he argued.

"Where is she? I need it off. It has to come off!" Gabriela attempted to pull herself away from Seth.

"Please…" her cries changed to pleas when Kara and his father finally entered the room.

"Hi Gabriela, how are you feeling?" she asked. Between hearing her shouting from the other room and the look on her face, she could tell that the future luna was not happy.

"Why would you do this? I said not to."

"I couldn't… I'm sorry. I had to treat it. I would've avoided it if I could, but unfortunately, the break was so severe that I had no choice." Kara walked over to her and led her back to the cot. "I promised I wouldn't ask so I won't." Grabbing a pen and pad, she wrote down some information on it before handing it to her. "This is my contact information. You will need to see me in six weeks for a checkup. Hopefully by then, the cast can come off."

The rest of the visit went quickly while Kara quietly filled her in on the rest of her findings from the x-ray. She whispered her results so that Gabriela could feel the sense of privacy even though Seth and his father could hear every detail. Once they were finished, she gave her a light hug before sending her on her way. Seth and his father walked with her to her locker in silence. Neither one of them knew what to say. Kara had made it very clear to the both of them that she was timid and would open up if and when she was ready.

"Um…thank you for looking out for me, Seth. I'm sorry for how I treated you earlier." She looked down at her feet. She knew he only wanted to help her.

"No problem. My dad and I are big about helping people who need it."

She smiled at them both. "What period are we in? I still have to go get my books from class."

"School's over. The teacher brought your books to the nurse's station. Grab the rest of your things… Seth and I can drop you home."

"Over? What time is it?" she asked in a panicked tone.

"Just past five," answered his dad.

"Thank you for the offer, sir, but my uncle said he was picking me up." She grabbed her book bag from Seth.

"Please, call me Justin, and as for your uncle… he came in looking for you. I already sent him home."

Gabriela's heart sunk. She had broken three of her uncle's rules on the first day of school. She felt her heartbeat increase as she nervously followed Seth and Justin to the exit of the school. She knew that in front of company, her uncle was the nicest person ever until they were alone.

"Would you like something to eat before I drop you home?" Justin asked. "You've been in the nurse's station all day I hear."

Gabriela shook her head. "No thank you, sir. I really should get home. My uncle will be looking for me."

"I told you to call me Justin. Please," he smiled at her as she followed him down the school steps.

Seth reached for Gabriela's book bag but stopped when he noticed a car pulling into the parking lot. Sensing his mate's discomfort, he mind-linked his father to let him know that this was the uncle that he had encountered earlier that morning. Gabriela shifted her weight from foot to foot as she waited for her uncle to exit the vehicle. When he finally stepped out of the car, she cringed at his voice and quickly put her arm behind her back.

"There you are! Your aunt and I were getting worried… I thought I told you I would pick you up." He shot a fake smile at his niece. "Get in. We have a lot to get done."

"Yes, Uncle," she answered. "Thank you for the offer, sir. Bye, Seth." She scurried down the steps to her uncle's car. Once inside the car, she smiled at Seth through the window before driving away.

Chapter 5

Gabriela was lying on the floor of her room when she woke up. Her uncle wasted no time attacking her as soon as they walked through the front door of their house the night before. Her scalp was sore from him pulling her up the stairs by her hair. Her uncle was furious that she had disobeyed his orders. Ignoring the screams of her aching body, she slowly climbed to her feet. She needed to shower and get out of the house as soon as possible before her uncle arrived. Since they had moved, he'd been keeping odd hours at his new place of work.

Once she was done her business in the bathroom, she quickly dressed herself and headed downstairs. Her uncle had told her toward the end of her beating that if he was home before she left for school, he would be driving her to school from now on.

Not wanting to wake her aunt, she snuck out of the house with her backpack over one shoulder. Gabriela decided to walk behind the houses along the tree line. Her uncle should come barreling down the road any minute, and that was the last thing she wanted. Almost right on cue, a pair of headlights sped down the street and skid to a stop in front of her house. She ducked down out of sight and backed herself quietly into past the tree line into the woods.

"Gabriela! Time for quality time before school!" she heard him yell as he swung the door open. "Gabriela!" he yelled, causing her to flinch at the tone in his voice.

She began to back herself deeper into the woods until the back door to the house swung open, forcing her to freeze, ducking down in fear. She held her breath as she heard her uncle's steps on the back patio. After what seemed like an eternity, her uncle's footsteps faded, and the door closed again.

Letting out a sigh of relief, Gabriela sprinted away from the house when she heard her uncle's yell again. She ran until her legs couldn't carry her anymore. She collapsed to her knees from a mixture of fear, exhaustion, relief, and pain and leaned back against a tree. Fear that her uncle would come rushing through the brush after her. Exhaustion from running as far and fast her legs would carry her. Relief that she managed to get away without being caught, and pain from her beating the night before. She shook her head to try and keep her fears at bay until she could catch her breath.

Gabriela reached into her book bag and pulled out a banana to eat when she heard a twig snap. She strained her eyes to see through the still dark woods when a pair of glowing blue eyes appeared a few feet in front of her. Gabriela let out a gasp as the glowing eyes came closer into view, along with the body of a large wolf.

"Oh god," she whispered as she pressed herself into the tree she was leaning against, squeezing her eyes shut. She figured that if the wolf was going to kill her, she didn't want to see it coming. Her breath hitched in her throat as she could hear the breath of the wolf getting closer each second until she could feel its breath near her face.

"Oh god," she said again, quieter than the first time followed by a squeal when the wolf did the one thing that she least expected…it licked her.

She opened her eyes to see the enormous wolf crouched down in front of her with its ears back and its head in its paws. She slowly held her hand out in front of her body toward the wolf. She wanted to let it smell her. Maybe, it was just curious. *Maybe, after it smells me and decides I taste nasty, it won't eat me,* she thought to herself. She smiled when the wolf licked her hand and crawled closer in its crouching position so that its head was lying in her lap.

"Thank you for not eating me," she said jokingly. "I'm sure I taste disgusting." She stroked its soft fur as she looked around. "You're cute… I wish I could take you home." She sighed as the wolf rolled over, exposing his belly to her. "But if I showed up with you, I'm sure my uncle would do more than just break my arm this time."

The wolf growled as soon as she made the comment about her uncle, causing Gabriela to pull her hand back. When the wolf stuck his tongue out and rolled on its side, she smiled. "You don't like my uncle either, huh?"

She giggled as the wolf shook its head from side to side as if to answer her question.

Seth

He sat outside of Gabriela's house in his wolf form. He had to beg his father to let him go to her house the next morning to escort her to school if she was going to walk. He couldn't quite figure his mate out, and that bothered him. She was so quiet and almost didn't speak. Once he and his father got her comfortable enough to talk to them, her asshole of an uncle showed up and stole her away…but what bothered him was the look of fear in her face as he watched them pull away.

His ears pricked as he heard the sound of a door opening and closing. He quietly prowled toward the side of his mate's house and watched her sneaking out of the house. He watched as his mate snuck into the woods a few yards down from where he watched. Why wouldn't she walk on the sidewalk? Why go in the woods? Being careful not to be seen, he snuck closer to her. He felt unsettled that his mate was walking through the woods this early in the morning…the sun wasn't even up yet. He crouched down on all fours as he heard his mate's heartbeat increase and her footsteps pick up further into the woods. He watched her duck down out of sight and make her past the tree line into the woods.

"Gabriela! Time for quality time before school!" he heard her uncle yelling. "Gabriela!" he yelled again.

He let out a low growl. He could sense that he meant his mate nothing but harm. He could smell the fear radiating from her. Once his mate took off running through the woods, he followed her at a safe distance. He wanted to be with her so badly, but he also knew that his huge wolf would scare her.

Once his mate settled near a tree, his wolf overpowered the little self-control that he had and walked him through the brush where she was. His mate.

"Oh god," he heard her whisper as he cautiously walked toward his mate. He whimpered as she tried to shrink herself into a tree, squeezing her eyes shut. "Oh god," she said again when he licked her.

He made himself as small as he could. He didn't want his mate to be afraid of him. "Thank you for not eating me," she said to him. "I'm sure I taste disgusting." He purred happily as she stroked his fur. "You're cute… I wish I could take you home."

Getting comfortable with his mate, he rolled over so that his mate could rub his belly. "But if I showed up with you, I'm sure my uncle would do more than just break my arm this time."

Seth growled at her confession to him about her uncle. Realizing that he had scared her, he rolled on his side before mind-linking his dad.

Dad... I was right. He does treat her badly. Worse than we thought.

How bad is it, Seth? he responded through the link.

She told me that her uncle broke her arm.

That's great that you got her to trust you so soon son! Now we can—

She doesn't trust me...not all of me, he confessed. *I'm in wolf form...but she's not afraid of me,* he said proudly through the link.

We will discuss that later. His father was angry.

Humans aren't supposed to see them in their wolf forms at all. Even though Gabriela was Seth's mate, he hadn't been introduced to her as her mate, which meant she still was considered an outsider to their pack.

Okay, Dad. I'm sorry. I know I broke the rules, but my wolf...he just overpowered me, he confessed to his dad as he curled himself protectively around his now sleeping mate. He knew that there was still plenty of time before school, and he could see the exhaustion in his mate's face.

Get her to the school. We can contact the human authorities and have them generate an investigation. I don't want her uncle showing up.

Seth closed the mind link. He hated to wake up his mate when she looked so peaceful. He began to lick her arm, causing her to stir. He nudged her with his wet nose when she smiled.

"Good morning," she said to him, stroking his head as she yawned. "I know you have no idea what I've been saying, but thank you for not eating me while I slept. I have to go now though. I can't be late for school." She stood up and dusted herself off with a smile as Seth whined in protest.

"Why are you whining? You don't have to go to school." She grabbed her pack off the ground and looked around. "God, I'm lost."

Seth nudged her leg gently. He stood up on all fours and licked her hand before tugging her pack a little. He was trying to convince her to follow him so he could lead her to school through the woods. After a few attempts, she understood that he wanted her to follow him.

The two walked side by side in silence for a while until Gabriela spoke. "Even though you can't understand…thank you, wolf." She stroked Seth's fur as they walked. Once they made it to the tree line at the school parking lot, she sighed.

"Bye wolf! Wish me luck!" She gave Seth one last rub before stepping through the tree line.

Seth whimpered loudly so that this mate could hear his sadness as she walked away toward the school. He was tempted to follow her past the woods if he knew his dad wouldn't kill him for it. He let out another whimper that turned into a howl. When Gabriela turned around and smiled at him, he felt his tail wag at his mate. He stood guard at the tree line until she disappeared inside the school.

Dad, she's in school. I linked Jace to watch over her while I'm with you. See you soon.

He linked Jace and the rest of the pack to keep an eye on his mate while he was with his dad contacting the human authorities regarding Gabriela's uncle. He wanted his mate with him, but her uncle was an obstacle in his way that needed to be dealt with.

Chapter 6

Gabriela fidgeted with her cast as she sat in her class. Even though her uncle forbade it, she was eager to see Seth for some reason that she couldn't understand. Her stomach was in knots every time a student would enter the classroom door. When the attendance bell went off, she let out a sad sigh. Seth was not in class.

"Hey! Gabi!" whispered Jace as the teacher was giving his lecture. "How's the arm?" He was sitting in the seat next to her. When she didn't answer, he leaned closer to her. "Hey…so I was thinking, you should sit with me and my friends at lunch."

Gabriela shook her head, never making eye contact with him. Even though her uncle specifically told her to stay away from Seth, she knew that he didn't want her conversing with anyone. Choosing to ignore Jace's constant attempts at a conversation, she flipped through the notes that the teacher was kind enough to copy for her since her dominant hand was casted.

Jace retreated from leaning toward her and mind-linked Seth. *Dude, she doesn't talk. How am I supposed to keep an eye on her when she won't speak to me?*

Follow her if you have to, but make sure she doesn't leave your sight or the school, he responded.

Jace looked over at his friend's mate to try and formulate a new plan. Class was nearly finished, and he needed to find some excuse to stick to her like glue. As soon as the bell rang, he followed her quickly out of the class.

"Hey! Gabriela…wait up!" he called down the hall as he caught up to her. "Here, I can help you with your books," he offered.

"No thanks… I'm okay." She looked around the hall cautiously as if she expected to see her uncle there waiting for her to disobey him again.

"Um, since we have the same class…how about we at least walk together?" he asked. He tried to follow her gaze as she looked around the hallways. "Are you looking for someone?"

"Um…no…sorry. I just…never mind," she stammered. "Um…thanks for offering, but I can't."

"Look…it's just that my friend, Seth, he really likes you, and he asked me to keep an eye out for you while he's out today," he confessed.

Gabriela smiled at his confession. "Why would he ask you to do that?"

"Let's just say he's very protective when he likes someone." He grinned as they neared their next class. "Oh… I guess I walked you to class after all, huh?" he chuckled as he held the door open for her.

Seth

Seth paced back and forth in his father's office. Justin was on the phone with the mate of one of his pack members. She was an officer with a nearby police station. When Justin hung up with the pack member's mate, he let out a long sigh.

"Seth, this is going to be harder than we thought." He leaned back in his chair. "Have a seat, son." He waited for Seth to take a seat across from him at his desk before continuing. "She told me what we need to do, but you won't like it any more than I do."

"Why? What'd she say?" he asked. He glanced at his cell phone. He was hoping to be at school by now with his mate instead of stuck listening to his dad's never-ending phone calls.

"Unfortunately, since your mate and her family are humans, we have to do this their way."

"We did! We called them, reported him…we're done. What's the problem?" Seth asked as he raked his hand through his hair.

"Proof. They need proof that she's being abused. Otherwise, they can't help."

"Dad, you saw her x-rays and the bruises! She confessed to me!"

"No!" he growled. "She didn't confess to you, she confessed to your wolf! A wolf that she should have never seen yet!" He banged his fist on his desk. "The x-rays and bruises are enough to open an inquiry, but she said it's not enough to get an emergency removal. She said unless she confesses to us as humans, he will need to be caught in the act."

"So we have to sit around and wait for her to show up with more bruises? Or broken bones?" Seth stood up in frustration. "School's almost over. I need to get there before she leaves."

"Head to the school but don't interfere. And for the love of the goddess, stay out of sight unless absolutely necessary," he commanded in his alpha tone.

Seth nodded at his father before heading out of the door. Once outside of the pack house, he mindlinked Jace. *Hey, change of plans…keep her busy until I get there.* He knew that his father gave him a direct order not to interfere but he did so as an alpha, not as his father. *And no matter what happens, don't tell my dad.*

Chapter 7

Seth rushed into the school and made his way to the cafeteria where Jace said that he and the rest of his pack were sitting with his mate. As he walked into the room, he took a deep breath, inhaling the scent of his mate. He closed his eyes as he let her scent calm his nerves when he heard a voice in front of him.

"Welcome back, Alpha," purred Jessica.

"I'm not in the mood. Move," he ordered as his eyes scanned the cafeteria for his mate.

"Why? Because the new human caught the eye of the Alpha? You're acting like the little human is your mate or something." She pouted.

"That's because she is," he growled. "She is my mate and will be your luna. You will change your attitude toward her, Jessica. And for the record, what you and I had is over, so stop coming on to me," he growled as he pushed past her toward Gabriela and the rest of his pack without giving Jessica a second glance. He grinned as he approached her.

She sat toward the edge of the table near the wall, with her face in a book.

"Hey, Gabi…how are you?" he breathed as he took the seat next to her.

"Seth, um…hi." She blushed as she scooted closer to the wall. Her eyes darted around the cafeteria as a precaution. "What are you doing here?"

"I go to school here." He laughed. He noticed her looking around the cafeteria and did the same. "Are we looking for someone?" he asked.

"No. Um…nice to see you, but I, uh, I have to go." She stood up from the table to leave.

"Wait, what's the rush?" He grabbed her left arm gently but tight enough to keep her from running away. His wolf purred in approval at the tingles from him touching her. "Is something wrong?" The panicked look on her face made him want to pull her into a hug.

"Nothing… I just forgot something in my locker."

He used his wolf hearing to listen to her heartbeat. Her pulse was fast. Too fast. Human pulses this fast were only like that if they had just finished exercising or from anger or fear. Recalling his father's words about her needing to confess about her situation or catch her being beaten, he adjusted his grip to her hand and gently led her out of the cafeteria. "Here, I'll walk with you." His words came out more as a command than a request or an offer. He listened to her pulse slow as they neared her locker.

"Hey, Gabi… I've been wanting to talk to you." He turned her to face him but frowned when her gaze was locked on the floor. "Gabi, please look at me."

"I can't, Seth…" She squeezed her eyes close as he lifted her chin.

"Open your eyes." His plea to her almost sounded as if he was in pain. "Please…it's okay." When she slowly opened her eyes, he purred to her. "That's better."

They stared at each other in silence before she spoke. "Seth…your eyes," she whispered. They looked familiar to her. She was lost in his gaze until a voice shattered the trance that they both were in.

"Gabriela!"

She spun around and gasped in fear. "Uncle!"

Without sparing Seth a glance, he stormed toward them and grabbed her by the arm. "We are leaving. Let's go!"

"Hey! You can't just—"

"Shut up, boy! I warned you to stay away from her," he hissed, interrupting Seth's protests. "Let's go!" he shouted again as he dragged Gabriela away. "Wait until I get you home," he whispered in her ear as he pulled her closer to him. "Your aunt has something to tell you."

Gabriela looked back over her shoulder as her uncle continued to force her toward the exit. *He might just go too far*, she thought as she took a mental image of the only friend she had disappear as they rounded the corner to the front doors of the school.

Gabriela and her uncle pulled up to the house a short time later after he pulled her from the school. She quietly exited the vehicle and hurried up the stairs. Not only had he warned her to stay away from him, he had warned him as well. Once inside the house, she found her aunt lying on the floor covered in cuts and bruises.

"Aunt Karina!" She rushed over to her and dropped to her knees. As much as she hated her for not intervening when her uncle would beat her, she hated to see her in such bad shape. "Aunt Karina!"

"Run, Gabi…run…" She groaned as she struggled to breathe. Gabriela helped her aunt to a sitting position. "You need to leave. The deal that Diego—"

"Shut up!" yelled her uncle.

"Diego, please…you don't have to do this," pleaded Karina.

"But I do, my dear wife…we had a deal."

"What deal?" Gabriela asked quietly.

"You see, dear niece. I loved your mother. I was in love with your mother…and you know what she did? She ran off with my best friend!" He walked over to the counter and poured himself a drink as he continued his story. "I had no choice to marry your aunt here, but unfortunately, your aunt knew…she knew everything, and when your parents died, that was my second chance."

Gabriela looked between her aunt and uncle. She didn't understand what he was talking about. "I don't understand. Second chance for what?"

"You see, you look just like your mother." He bent down and ran a finger down her cheek. "Your aunt caught me looking at you the way I looked at your mother, so I made her a deal."

Gabriela gasped when the realization of what he was saying hit her.

"I promised not to touch you if your aunt promised not to interfere. But the deal's off. Your aunt tried to stop me from coming to get you today from school, and here we are."

Gabriela looked at her aunt with tear-filled eyes. "I'm so sorry… I didn't know," she cried. She felt guilty for all the things she had said to her when she was only trying to protect her from her uncle's true intentions. She leaned down to hug her aunt before being ripped off her.

"Since the deal is no longer valid…you and I have some business to discuss!" He dragged her away from her aunt and threw her to the floor in the living room, causing her to fall into and break the living room coffee table. As Gabriela tried to roll over and crawl away, he grabbed her ankle and yanked her back. "I've waited so long to do this," he growled as he ripped her shirt open, exposing her bra. He ripped his own shirt open and undid his belt and pants as she attempted to crawl away a second time. He kicked her in the ribs and rolled her to her back, holding her arms above her head while he started to pull and tug at her pants.

"Please…don't do this…please!" Her pleas fell on deaf ears as she struggled against him. Once she felt him trying to put his knee between her legs, she let out a bloodcurdling scream, causing him to punch her so hard that black dots danced across her blurry vision.

"Shut up!" he hissed. "I promise you will enjoy what I'm about to do to you."

"Please…no," she begged again as she struggled against his weight.

"I said shut up!" he yelled as he punched her again.

Gabriela sobbed quietly as she squeezed her eyes shut. She couldn't struggle much longer. Her body was weakening. Right when she felt him push her legs open, she heard a loud crash before hearing a familiar voice.

"What the fuck?" Diego let go of Gabriela's arms as he watched Seth and Justin follow a group of police officers through the front door.

"Get off of her and put your hands up!" ordered a female officer. The officer approached Gabriela as another officer grabbed Diego and handcuffed him.

"Hey, Gabi…can you hear me?" Seth said to her softly. He pulled his shirt off over his head and placed it over her to cover her nearly naked body. "Gabi, please…open your eyes for me. Come on, Kitten," he begged. He pulled her body into his, placing his forehead against hers. "Kitten, I need you to open your eyes."

"Seth, the paramedics are here. You need to let her go." The female officer reached out for his mate but pulled back when Seth let out a possessive growl over his mate. "Seth…she needs medical attention." She reached for her again but was met with the same result. "Alpha," she called to Justin.

"Son, you're wasting precious time. They need to take her now." Justin knew that reasoning with his son wasn't the problem. The problem was with Seth's wolf. Wolves were already possessive territorial animals, but alpha wolves were twice as possessive. He bent down near Seth who let out another loud possessive growl at him. His eyes were completely black. "Seth…your mate needs help. Look at her, she needs a doctor," he said to Seth in his alpha tone, looking him in the eyes.

Seth growled at him as he reached for Gabriela, but it wasn't as loud as before. Without breaking eye contact, he pulled her from his grasp, ignoring Seth's growls.

The female officer and another officer grabbed her from Justin's arms. "Thank you, Alpha," she said as they rushed her out of the house to a stretcher waiting nearby.

Seth and Justin followed them out of the house and watched as they began to take her vitals and start an IV. When one of the paramedics lifted Seth's shirt to put stickers for the heart monitors, another growl erupted from him, causing the paramedic to freeze in fear.

"Son, please...let them do their job." Justin gripped Seth's arms as he tried to pull free to reach his mate.

"He shouldn't be looking at her like that. She's mine! My mate!" he growled as his wolf began to regain control over his body.

"Calm down, Seth, I know she's your mate! He's helping her. Control your wolf!" he ordered.

Seth's eyes returned back to their blue color. Once she was loaded in the back of the ambulance, he turned to see another stretcher being put in another ambulance nearby. "I need to go with her."

"We can meet them there," replied Justin.

As much as Seth wanted to be in the ambulance, he knew that was the worst place for a possessive alpha werewolf with an injured mate. He and Seth rushed down the driveway to his vehicle. Seth opened his mouth to protest but nothing came out. His dad was right. He was wrong to think that he would've been able to control himself around his mate...especially after what he saw was happening to her. He needed her more than he ever thought possible. Justin pulled away from the house, passing the police cars along the road. Seth let out a growl as he watched her uncle slide into the back of a police cruiser. As much as he wanted to rip his throat out, that was for another day. His mate needed him.

Chapter 8

Beep.

   Beep.

   Beep.

Seth sat next to Gabriela as she laid in the hospital bed. His mate was going on the second day of being unconscious. The only thing that let him know that his mate was still breathing was the monitor beeping at the rate of her heartbeat. He hated himself for not realizing how bad her life was at home. He stroked her hand as he held it, longing for her to wake up so that he could apologize.

"I'm so sorry I let this happen to you," he said softly to her.

"You didn't let that happen to her…" He looked up to see who the voice belonged to. Karina, her aunt. "I did, and I'm so sorry," she sobbed as she approached the bed. "Look at what he did to you," she whispered.

Seth stood up in a protective stance. He wasn't sure what to make of Gabriela's battered and bruised aunt. She was crying over what her husband did to her, but did she try and stop him before? He narrowed his eyes before speaking, "She has cracked ribs, and he fractured one arm…broke the other that was already in a cast." Karina winced at Seth's words, but he continued. "How long?" he asked her. "How long was he beating her like this?"

"For a while," she responded. She walked up to the bed and stroked Gabriela's hair. "For too long," she added. A tear slid down her cheek as she took a seat on the opposite side from where Seth stood.

"For a while? You let that bastard beat her like this? Do you have any idea how many old injuries the doctor found?"

"I know that you don't understand, but—"

"You're right! I don't understand!" he roared. "He was trying to rape her! Do you have any idea how close he was? How close he got? What would've happened if we would've showed up a second later?"

"If you would just let me explain," she begged. Karina had planned on coming to Gabriela's room to explain to her how things got so out of hand with Diego.

"You can't explain this!" he hissed. "Nothing you can say can explain what me and my dad saw when we walked in your house!"

"Don't you dare lecture me!" she cried. "You have no idea about the choices I made to keep today from happening!"

Seth took a step toward Karina to respond but stopped when a quiet voice interrupted him. "Stop...don't fight," came Gabriela's raspy voice. She squinted her eyes at the brightness in the white room. "Please, don't."

"You're awake!" Seth pulled his chair closer to the bed and sat down, taking her hand in his. "Let me call the nurse for you." He reached for the nurse's button before grabbing a cup of water. "Are you thirsty?" Not waiting for her answer, he lifted the cup to her lips so that she could take a sip.

Gabriela cleared her dry throat. "Did...did he—" She choked back a cry as she tried to finish the sentence that she dreaded the answer to.

Seth winced as she struggled with what she was asking. "No, Kitten, he didn't. The uh...the doctors said—"

"The doctors said you're going to be fine," interrupted Karina as Seth glared at her. Another tear slid down her cheek as she watched Gabriela let out a sigh of relief. "Gabi... I owe you an apology and explanation."

"You sure do," spat Seth as he continued to glare at Karina.

"Seth...please," Gabriela pleaded with him. "Let her speak." He huffed in response.

"Your Uncle Diego...he was in love with your mother. So much that he thought that she would leave your father for him if he broke up with me.

He was obsessed." She closed her eyes and took a deep breath before continuing. "When your mother told him no, she came and told me what he wanted to do. At first, I didn't believe her, but after a while when his behavior began to change... I saw she was right. You were four by then. Not too long after, your parents died in an accident. You came to live with us...everything was fine until you were nine. I caught him in your bedroom. He was watching you sleep...the look on his face...it wasn't how you look at your niece."

"Why the hell didn't you leave then?" asked Seth. Feeling his wolf trying to surface, he closed his eyes and took a breath of his mate's scent to soothe him. He could tell that this was going to be a difficult story to hear.

"Seth, let her talk," Gabriela's voice was a little louder than a whisper but firm enough to snap him and his wolf back to control.

"That's what you don't understand," Karina said to Seth. "I did leave! I took her, and I ran! I pulled Gabi from school when he was at work and took off. He found us after three days, then I ran again... and again...but he always found us." She looked at Gabriela with apologetic eyes. "He has friends in high places...high enough that when I called the police the first time he beat you, Gabriela...instead of me. The cops just laughed at me and told me to get them a beer!" she cried.

"I remember that," whispered Gabriela. "It was my birthday." She had always thought that those were dreams…nightmares of what would happen if she ran away.

"That day in front of them, he said he promised to beat you only instead of…" her voice trailed off, but she could see in Gabriela's face that she understood the deal she made. Beatings daily in order for her to keep her virtue…her virginity. "That day when you left for school, he came home drunk… with that look in his eyes. The same look he used to have when he looked at your mother. I saw that look, and I knew that we had to go, so when I tried to talk him out of going to get you from school, he beat me, and well…you know the rest."

Gabriela swallowed down a lump in her throat. "What happened to him? Where is he?"

Seth frowned. He could see the fear in her eyes. The increasing beeps from the monitor announced her panic to the room.

"Shhhh, Kitten, calm down." When the beeping continued to increase, he pressed the call button for the nurse again. Only then did he realize that the nurse never came in on the first call.

Within seconds, a handful of nurses and a doctor came rushing into the room. "Miss…can you hear me?" The doctor approached her and flashed a light in her eyes. "She's having a panic attack," announced the doctor.

"I'm sorry, both of you are going to have to leave…" said a nurse. When neither Karina nor Seth moved, she spoke again, "You both need to leave. I promise you can come back and see her when she's stable."

Seth began to back away slowly as she watched the nurses administer a couple different medications into Gabriela's IV. His heart ached as she watched her thrashing about in the bed before the sound of her slowing heart rate from the monitor filled the room. His mate was still afraid of a man that was now behind bars. The fact that he was still breathing enraged him. He followed Karina out in the hall and took a seat beside her.

"I don't expect you to understand the choices I made to raise her," she said softly as she looked down at her fingers. "Gabi doesn't know this, but I tried everything to get her placed in a different home… when her mother made me promise to protect her, I knew protecting her meant sending her away, but he had some judge change the order. He flat-out told me that I had no right to make a decision like that without him, and he showed up with her a day later."

Seth looked at the closed hospital door as Karina's words sunk in. "So you're telling me he's going to get out?"

She nodded. "He's going to get out…he always does. And when he does, he's going to come for her." She looked at Seth with tear-filled eyes. "He's going to come for her and kill anyone who gets in his way…"

Chapter 9

"Really, sir, I mean Justin…you don't have to do all of this. I don't want to inconvenience you guys more than I already have," breathed Gabriela as Justin helped her out of the bed. Today, she was being discharged to go home.

"Shush, you will be coming home to stay with my family. We are happy to take you in." Justin smiled at his son's mate.

"What about Aunt Karina?"

"She is more than welcome to come, but she said she needed to get some stuff in order for you both. She will be there later in the week. She's waiting downstairs to see you." Justin grabbed the small bag of Gabriela's clothes and threw it over his shoulder. "I really think you should be in a wheelchair," he insisted as the two walked down the hall.

"I've been stuck in a bed for almost two weeks. I want to use my legs." She smiled as they approached the exit doors to the hospital where Seth was waiting with Karina. "It's so beautiful out." She took a deep breath and closed her eyes, enjoying the warmth of the sun on her skin.

"You shouldn't be walking, Kitten."

"Yes, I should." She said as she walked past him to her aunt. "Are you sure you can't come with us?" She and her aunt had grown closer since she was in the hospital. "We have so much to talk about...and we—"

"Gabi, I have to get some things your mom left for you. Once I have everything your mom left you shipped, you will be my first stop. I promise." She pulled her niece in for a hug. "Take care of her for me?" she said to Justin and Seth.

"No need to ask...she's already a part of the family," said Justin with a smile.

Karina gave one last brief hug before walking away, leaving Seth, Justin, and Gabriela standing by Justin's car. "You ready to see your new home?" asked Seth as he helped her into the car.

The drive was a long one. After almost an hour of driving, the car pulled up to an enormous house. Gabriela leaned forward in her seat to take a good look before unclicking her seat belt. "This is your house?" she asked.

"No...this is *our* house," responded Justin. "You live here now, which makes this just as much your house as it is ours. Come on, Seth will show you around."

Gabriela nodded as she followed Seth into the house. He reached for her hand, leading her around by her fingers since she now was sporting a full arm cast on one arm and a cast up to her forearm on the other. She silently made mental notes of each room he took her to. After showing her around on the first level, he guided her up the stairs.

"So this room here is going to be your room… my room is right next door, and Dad's is just down the hall," he said as he opened the door for her, pulling her inside gently. "It's not decorated… I didn't know what color you would've liked, so we left it plain. Tomorrow, if you feel up to it, we can go shopping and get what you need for your room and stuff."

"It's perfect," she said just above a whisper. She walked around the large room before pausing. "This is too much… I can't—"

"You can and you will." Seth crossed the room to where Gabriela stood. "You've been cheated out of a lot, but here, you are going to get everything you ever wanted…everything you could've wanted."

Gabriela blushed as she turned away to check out the closet and the bathroom. "I went back to your place and grabbed some clothes but you can buy some tomorrow when you buy stuff for your room too," he offered.

"Seth, I don't shop. That requires a lot of what I don't have," she said jokingly. "Uncle Diego never gave me any money… I can't repay you guys until I get better to get a job—"

"You're not getting a job," interrupted Justin's voice from the doorway. "You are going to take one of my cards and buy whatever you want." He pulled out his wallet and walked across to where Seth and Gabriela were standing. "Use this card for whatever you want. Once you're done, hang on to it just in case for emergencies."

"Thank you, Justin, I don't need much," she said as she accepted the card.

"You weren't listening," laughed Justin. "I didn't say what you needed… I said what you wanted, and make sure you shop. I hate shopping, so if you do it, I won't have to."

Gabriela giggled.

"Dinner's ready. You have a lot of people to meet." Justin led Gabriela and Seth back down the steps to the dining hall where a large group of people stood. She smiled nervously as she scanned the faces in the crowd. Some she recognized from school, but most were faces she'd never seen before.

"Everyone, this is Gabriela. She's Seth's class-*mate*," he said, phrasing the end of classmate differently. "I trust everyone will help her feel welcome and at home." Everyone nodded before approaching Gabriela to introduce themselves with smiling faces.

After mostly everyone has had a chance to speak with her, Justin announced that it was time to eat. Gabriela ate quietly as everyone else conversed around the table. Since she wasn't used to getting actual meals, after a few bites, she began to move the food around on her plate.

"Kitten? You okay?" asked Seth with concern.

"Yeah, I'm fine." She quickly looked around the room before giving him a small smile.

"You stopped eating," he said to her.

"Oh. I, uh, it's just that I'm full," she responded. She glanced around the table before lowering her voice to a whisper. "I normally don't," she paused before correcting herself. "I didn't get to eat regular meals… I'm not used to eating, that's all." She dropped her gaze to her fingers in embarrassment. When she realized the room went quiet, she looked up from her fingers to see that everyone in the room was staring at her.

Act normal like you didn't hear anything, commanded Justin. Even though she lowered her voice to whisper to Seth, everyone heard her response to him since everyone at the table except her had werewolf abilities, including super hearing. *Your future luna is not to be made uncomfortable.* Everyone at the table resumed eating and talking to each other.

"I, uh, can I be excused?" asked Gabriela to Justin.

"Of course, you don't have to ask here," he responded.

"Thank you, sir… Justin." She looked around at everyone at the table. "I'm just… I—"

"I understand. I will check on you after dinner." Justin gave her a smile before she left the room.

He used his super hearing to make sure that Gabriela was in her room before speaking again. He noticed Seth's grip on the armrests of the dinner chair. "Son, your mate is here in the house." Justin cleared his throat. "Your future luna is human. Everyone *will* keep control of their wolf. No one is to discuss pack business around or near her until she has been informed of our kind. Do I make myself clear?" he questioned.

"Yes, Alpha," responded everyone…everyone except Seth.

"Seth, do I make myself clear?" he asked again.

"Yeah, Dad," he breathed. Justin's alpha wolf let out a warning growl. "Yes, Alpha," he said.

"Now, go check on your mate," he ordered Seth.

Seth sprang out of his chair and out of the room. He could feel his wolf's mixture of feelings as it tried to come to terms with what Gabriela had shared with him at dinner. Anger that he learned that she wasn't fed normally. Sadness that his mate felt uncomfortable because of yet another thing her uncle did to her. He took a deep breath as he arrived at Gabriela's door. Using his wolf hearing, he could hear sobs and sniffles from the other side of the door.

"Kitten? It's Seth," he called to her as he knocked. "Gabi?" He knocked again. When he knocked a third time, he grabbed the handle. "Kitten, I'm coming in…okay?" He waited a few seconds before turning the knob. He poked his head through the door to a sight that made his wolf want to howl in pain. Gabriela was on the floor, with her back against the wall, crying, curled up in a ball.

"Kitten…what's wrong?" he asked as he went over and slid down beside her.

"Everything…everything's wrong." She sobbed. "I tried to sleep…but I can't," she choked out. "Every time I close my eyes, he's there!"

"Oh, Gabi," he pulled her into him and held her tight. "Shhhh, Kitten, it's okay."

Her body shook as she cried harder as he held her. "I can feel him touching me… I can see him!"

"Gabi, he's not here…he's in jail," he assured her as he rocked her back and forth.

He remembered the nurses telling his dad that she's been having nightmares and flashbacks from her attack and that she had been jumpy since her uncle tried to rape her. He rocked her back and forth until her breathing evened out. He lifted her up and carried her over to the bed to tuck her in under the covers.

As soon as he turned to leave, he heard her call out to him. "Seth?" she called softly. "Can you stay with me? Please?" she begged. "You help keep the nightmares away," she confessed, remembering how he would hold her hand whenever she would sleep if she began to have a flashback. Just him touching her would drive the dreams away.

Seth nodded at her. "Sure." He climbed into bed and pulled her into his chest and smiled. His wolf purred in excitement as he hugged her.

"Thank you, Seth, for everything that you and your dad are doing for me." She took a deep breath and snuggled into his chest, drifting off to sleep.

"Good night, Kitten…see you in the morning."

Chapter 10

"Wolf! What are you doing here?" Gabriela said as she opened her eyes to find the large wolf from the other day where Seth was sleeping when she fell asleep last night. She sat up from her bed and looked around as the large wolf laid his massive head on her lap. She stroked the top of his head. *"Your eyes look so familiar,"* she said to the wolf as he nuzzled his snout in between her casted arm and her waist.

"Gabi... Gabi," called Seth to her, gently shaking her from her sleep. "Gabi, wake up."

She opened her eyes and looked around cautiously before looking at Seth.

"Gabi? Are you okay? You were talking about a wolf in your sleep..." he mentioned to her with a grin. She opened her mouth to answer when a knock came from the other side of the door.

"Come in," called Seth.

"Hey, you two," said Justin as he walked in. "Good morning." He smiled.

"Oh my god, sir! It's not what it looks like!" Gabriela shot up from the bed but doubled over with a hiss. She forgot how badly her body was hurt and that she still had a long way to go before she was healed.

"Careful, Kitten," said Seth as he reached for her in concern.

"Don't worry, Gabi, relax. I know you two aren't doing anything. No need to panic." Justin assured her.

"But you walked into my room and your son is in my bed." She frowned. "I don't understand… most parents would be livid."

"Yes, but I'm not most parents…besides, you're a respectful girl. I can tell you aren't like that." Justin walked over to the dresser in the bedroom and laid some cash on it. "Breakfast is ready. Here's some money for when you guys go out. Always make sure you carry cash, understand? You never know when there might be an emergency." Gabriela nodded at him in response. "I'll see you both downstairs."

Gabriela watched as Justin walked out. "Thank you for staying with me," she said as she got out of the bed.

"Anytime…see you downstairs."

She watched him as he walked out before heading to the bathroom to do her business and get dressed. After a short while, she was dressed and headed down the stairs. She followed the smell of food through the halls until she made her way to the dining hall. She scanned the faces at the table, many who were there last night for dinner. She smiled as she walked in.

"There you are," said Seth. "Come on and eat… we have a lot to do today."

She hurried across the room to the chair next to Seth. She nibbled on a piece of bacon that Seth had placed on her plate before leaning over to whisper to him. "There's so many people here…is everyone here related to you?"

Seth chuckled. "My dad and I are big on friends and family…think of everyone now as your extended family." He smiled at her until he heard a scoff from the other end of the table. "Everyone except her…" He glared at Jessica who was glaring daggers at Gabriela.

"She's related to you?" asked Gabriela confused.

"It's complicated," he began. "I promise to tell you soon bu—" Seth froze when a howl sounded in the distance, interrupting him. Without warning, he shot out of his chair behind his father with all the other members following suit.

"Gabi, stay inside and away from the windows and doors," Justin ordered as everyone ran out of the front door.

"Wait! Where are you guys going? What's wrong?" she asked.

"Just stay here…please." added Seth before running out the door, slamming it behind him, leaving her alone in the house.

Gabriela stared at the door in shock until a bloodcurdling scream interrupted her thoughts. She ran through the house to a backsliding glass door where a little girl and boy huddled against a tree, clinging to each other not too far from the house. Without thinking, she slid the door open and ran toward the kids. She saw a pile of baseball bats and hockey sticks near the kids. She ran as fast as her legs would carry her, grabbing an aluminum bat on her way. She neared the kids, just as the large wolf was crouched down as if it were going to lunge for its prey. Just as the wolf lunged at the kids, she swung the bat, hitting it on the side of its massive head. She swung again at it, causing it to growl as she found her mark a second time. She stood protectively in front of the kids, gripping the bat as tight as she possibly could with two casted arms. When the wolf lunged again, she swung the bat only to have the wolf catch it in its teeth and toss it away with the shake of its head.

She felt the heat of its breath as it took another step toward them. Gabriela backed the kids as close to the tree as she could before turning her back to the wolf as if to shield them from it. Hugging them tightly, she closed her eyes right when a familiar howl sounded from the left of them. She looked over to see the same wolf that kept her company when she was lost heading to school. The brown wolf growled and changed his attention from her and the kids to the approaching wolf who came to stand between him, Gabriela, and the kids.

The brown wolf lunged without warning, causing Gabriela to yelp. "Wolf!" she cried as the two wolves clawed and snapped at each other. After what seemed like an eternity, the brown wolf let out a yip in pain and hobbled off with two wolves snapping its jaws close behind it. Gabriela's large black protector wolf turned to face her and the kids and approached her slowly with its head down. She held her hand out and touched his soft fur.

"Thank you, wolf," she said softly.

The wolf nudged her affectionately as she turned around, still clinging to the kids. Gabriela bent down to the kids and began to inspect them for injuries when she heard a variety of howls erupt from behind her. "Oh my god," she breathed. She stood protectively in front of the kids. "Stay behind me," she ordered them.

"It's okay, Luna," said the older of the two, pulling the other from behind her.

"No, it's not!" she shrieked, stepping back in front of the kids. She did her best to shield them with her body when the black wolf approached her and nudged her and the kids toward the door of the house. She looked at the black wolf and back up to the pack of huge wolves now standing behind her black protector and gasped in shock. All the wolves were crouched down with their ears back, just as the black wolf had done when she first met him.

"Kids, slowly head to the house…"

"But—" said the little boy again, gripping his sister's hand before shutting his mouth when one of the wolves growled.

"Just go, please? I will make you whatever you want…just go…now!" she urged.

She kept the kids behind her as she backed away slowly to the steps and into the house. Once they were inside, she slammed the door shut and locked it. She watched all the wolves get up from their crouching positions and prance away…all except for one. The black wolf stood up and seemed to bow his head to her before trotting off after the others. Not long after the wolves were gone, the front door opened, and a voice rang out through the house.

"Gabi! Gabi, where are you?" shouted Seth as he ran through the house to her. "What the hell were you doing outside? I told you to stay inside!" He pulled her into a tight hug and buried his face in the crook of her neck. "You could've been killed!"

Gabriela pulled out of Seth's hug. "So could they! What was I supposed to do? Let the wolf eat them?" she shrieked. "And where were you? After one showed up and scared one away, a whole pack of them showed up! You expected me to stay in the house with people outside? And how do you know I was outside? You weren't here and the kids—" she inhaled. "Oh my god! The kids!" She pushed past Seth toward the two children who stood off to the side.

"They're fine…their mother is on her way." He smiled as he watched Gabriela inspect the kids again for injuries. He was thankful that her worry for the kids distracted her from him having to answer how he knew that she was outside to begin with.

"Hey, I promised you guys whatever you want if you came in…what would you guys like?" she said softly to them.

Both kids looked past her at Seth questioningly before responding after he nodded to them in approval.

"Ice cream!" they yelled together.

"Ice cream it is," she said with a smile. "Go sit at the table until your mother gets here." She walked to the freezer and found a tub of Turkey Hill.

"Here, Kitten, let me do it. It's going to be hard doing things until you get those off." He took the tub from her while she grabbed two bowls and headed for the dining hall. He silently scooped two scoops in each bowl and watched his mate place a bowl in front of each kid.

Feeling Seth's eyes on her, she looked up. "What?" she asked quietly as she brushed the little girl's hair from her face.

"What you did today was brave," he said to her. "Stupid…but brave."

"So?" she responded. "I would do it again in a heartbeat if it meant no one got hurt. They had nowhere to run," she said as Justin entered the room that she could only assume to be the mother of the two children.

"Gabi, this is Kristen… Jackie and Jack's mother," said Justin, introducing them.

"Thank you so much, Lu—Gabriela for saving my kids," she said with tears in her eyes. She pulled her into a brief hug and thanked her again.

"Don't thank me," she said. "I did it because it was the right thing to do."

"I'm forever in your debt," she said as she walked over to her kids, pulling them into a hug.

"Look, Momma, Luna gave us ice cream," said the little boy.

Gabriela smiled. "It looks like I have a nickname," she said to Seth.

"Oh, you have no idea." He grinned at her before looking at his dad.

"Son, maybe you should get Gabi out of the house. Go shopping. I will see you two when you get back."

Seth nodded. He told Gabriela that he was going to get the car and that he would be waiting for her out front. Gabriela crouched down to the eye level of the two little kids. "Hey, guys, I have to go… do me a favor and stay away from big bad wolves for me, okay?" she said with a smile.

"Yes, Luna," they both replied in unison.

Gabriela let out a small giggle. "My name is Gabriela...you guys can call me Gabi. Okay?"

"Yes, Luna Gabi," they replied in unison again.

She opened her mouth to respond but gave up when she heard Seth blow the horn. "Never mind," she said with a chuckle. "Thank you, sir, uh, Justin." She reached up on her toes and gave him a kiss on the cheek before heading out of the room and out of the door.

Chapter 11

Justin waited to hear Seth's car pull away before speaking. "Kristen, have them checked out by the pack doctor," he ordered.

"Yes, Alpha." She bowed her head as he walked past her and out of the room.

Justin walked back outside to the back of the house where most of his pack were gathered. "Today was too close of a call," he announced. "A rogue made it close enough to the pack house to try and attack two pups and your future luna!" he roared. He looked at all the faces before him before continuing, "Can anyone explain to me how a rogue made it this close to the house?"

He was furious. His pack was trained better than this. The two biggest rules have been broken… to protect the borders of their pack and the pack house where the luna resided.

"Alpha, it appears the rogues came through undetected in between our pack and the neighboring pack," said Justin's beta. Chris cleared his throat before responding. "We tracked their scent from the border to every entry point of the house."

Justin let out a growl. "Have the warriors do a perimeter check." He turned toward the house and headed up to his office with Chris close behind. Once they were behind the closed doors of his office, he growled again. "Only pack members know that the border between here and the other pack is unguarded because of how close it is. How would they know to look there?"

"Think someone told them?" Chris questioned out loud. It wasn't uncommon for scorned pack members turned rogue to expose weaknesses to pack enemies.

"But who? We only stopped guarding that point within the last month!" He ran his hands through his hair. That meant they had a traitor among them…a current one. "What did the rogue say?"

"Just that he's here to seal the deal so the trade can be made…he's making no sense."

"Keep questioning him and double the security. It bothers me that they went straight for the house. No one was in here except Gabi." He stood up from his desk and walked over to the window. He wondered if the rogues were after the future luna of the pack, but if they were, how would they know that Seth found his mate? She wasn't formally introduced as the future luna yet except for the members who were present for dinner. "Do you think they were after her?"

"I don't know, Alpha, but if they were, she'll give them a run for their money. She stood her ground against a rogue! She's a human!"

Justin smiled. "She's a brave one," he added. "It's a shame how she's been treated. Speaking of her, when is her uncle's court date?"

"Monday, his lawyer is petitioning the court for bail." Chris grabbed the tablet from Justin's desk and pulled up Diego's criminal charges on the public record site. "They won't give him bail, right?"

"I would like to think they won't. We literally walked in on him trying to rape her," growled Justin. "I can't see how any judge would allow him out." He grimaced as he recalled the painful sight he and Seth saw when they walked into Gabriela's house.

"Alpha, everything will be okay. Everything always works itself out," assured Chris. He could see the pain in his face.

"I hope you're right… I don't think that poor girl can take any more heartache," he said. "Come on…let's go see the rogue."

*****

"Come on, Kitten! There's no way that this is all you're buying," Seth said as he pulled her through the mall.

"Seth…please. I don't need to buy all this stuff." She pulled against him in protest. They had already visited a few furniture stores before heading to the mall to shop for clothes. "We have enough."

"No, Kitten. I have enough. I bought most of the stuff we have. You have one bag of clothes!"

"I don't need more than this. Your dad—"

"My dad said buy what you want…not what you need."

Gabriela sighed as Seth pulled her toward Victoria's Secret. "You are insane if you think we're going in there together."

"I promise to behave," he said with a smile as he pushed her inside.

He walked around with her for a while before flagging down a store employee to take her into a changing room so she could be measured and be more comfortable picking out her undergarments. Once she was out of sight, he pulled out his cell to text his dad. He wanted to know what his dad learned from the interrogation with the rogue. After sending a few texts, he walked over to some of the scented spray to see if he could find one that Gabriela might like. He grabbed a couple and turned toward the changing room when Jessica bumped into him.

"Fancy seeing you here, Seth," purred Jessica. "You hate shopping," she pointed out to him.

"No, Jessica. I hated shopping with you. I actually like shopping with my mate." He rolled his eyes as he sidestepped her and continued his way back to where Gabriela should emerge shortly.

"How is your mate after today's close call? She wasn't too shaken, was she?"

Seth could hear the obvious sarcasm in Jessica's voice, making her fake concern apparent. "Jessica, what do you want?"

"I want what's best for our pack, Alpha," she said seductively. "Today's attack proves that a human can't be your luna. She's weak and doesn't have what it takes to stand by you and lead the pack like I can."

Seth turned to her and growled. "Gabi *will* be the luna...*my* luna. Today, she proved herself not only to be worthy to me but to the whole pack. She ran into danger for someone else!" he hissed quietly so that no human could hear. "She, as a human, was willing to put her life before two pups that were complete strangers to her in front of a rogue and a whole pack of wolves!" He made no attempt to hide his eyes that were now black. His wolf was furious that she would dare talk like that about his mate.

Jessica frowned and bowed her head in submission. This was not at all how she planned this conversation would go. Her wolf whimpered. She could sense that whatever romantic feelings Seth had toward her before Gabriela showed up were long gone. Only when Seth took a step back from her did she regain her composure, standing up straight. She watched him turn toward Gabriela who emerged from the back room with an employee and a basket of garments. Jealousy and anger flooded through her body as she watched Seth rush to his mate. Just as they were going to pass her, she plastered a fake smile on her face when they approached.

"Hi, Jessica," said Gabriela. "How are you?"

"I've been better," she responded in a cold tone. She opened her mouth to say something else but thought better of it when she saw Seth's eyes changing from blue to black.

"I'm sorry to hear that. We are about to have lunch. Do you want to come with?" she asked Jessica with a smile.

"No… I'm good. I gotta go anyway." She put the clothes that she had in her hands on a nearby shelf and walked away from them.

"She hates me," Gabriela said as they placed their items on the counter.

"Nah, she hates everyone." Seth grabbed the bag from the counter and led the way out of the store. "Even though you didn't buy a lot, I think we should head home. It's getting late."

"Speaking of heading home…you've been avoiding my questions about today since we've been out today." Gabriela looked at Seth, waiting for him to answer. Since they left the house and for most of the day, she tried to talk to Seth about what happened with the wolves.

"I'm not avoiding anything, Kitten." He popped the trunk and placed the bags inside. "There's just not much to say," he said, quickly getting into the driver's side.

"Seth, you guys have a serious wolf problem!" she shrieked as they pulled away from the mall.

"Says the girl who was talking to one," he replied.

He tap-danced around the wolf conversation all day. He wanted to tell her about him and his pack over time, but with today's attack, he worried he would have to do it sooner. He wasn't sure how she would take living with a pack of wolves...especially after one tried to attack her.

"Let's just get home. We can talk about it over dinner, I promise."

Later that night, dinner at the pack house was quiet. Gabriela looked awkwardly around the room at everyone before settling her gaze on her plate. She wanted to say something about the wolves, but no one seemed bothered by it except for her.

Sensing her discomfort, Justin cleared his throat. "Did you find some things that you liked today?" he asked her.

"Yes, I did."

"No, she didn't," interrupted Seth. "I had to drag her to every store!"

"Because I didn't need all the stuff you wanted me to buy." She leaned back in her seat. "Besides,

I told you I needed school clothes…not the whole store."

Justin chuckled. "Speaking of school, Jace brought home the schoolwork you missed. They said you can go back when you're ready."

"Great…can I go Monday after his arraignment?" she asked, not wanting to say Diego's name.

"No, you can't," Seth growled out before Justin could answer.

"I wasn't asking you, Seth," she shot back. "You're not my guardian, your dad is…and since when do you think you can control what I do and make decisions for me?"

"Since I'm your ma—"

"Seth!" roared Justin. "That's enough!" His voice boomed as he slammed his hand on the table, causing Gabriela to flinch. Realizing the fear in her eyes, his eyes softened. "Gabi, I'm sorry. I didn't mean to scare you. Seth is only worried about you, that's all. You had a rough day today."

He looked at Seth for him to say something to his mate to comfort her. He understood Seth's concern for her safety after the rogue attack today, but since Gabriela didn't know anything about werewolves and mates, they couldn't explain his reasoning to her yet.

"Look, I'm sorry. It's just I really like you, and I feel protective over you," he admitted.

Gabriela looked around at everyone at the table. Everyone's gaze was down at their plates. "I think I'm going to call it a night. Thank you, guys, for today…" she said softly before standing up and exiting the room. She hurried up the stairs and into her room.

Chapter 12

Gabriela sat in the audience at the courthouse. It was already Monday, and she, Justin, and Seth had just come from getting her casts removed. She fidgeted nervously with her fingers as she waited for her uncle to be brought into the room. She hadn't seen him since the day he attacked and tried to rape her. A few moments later, a pair of side doors opened, and her uncle shuffled in the room with handcuffs and ankle shackles on. She felt the air leave her lungs as he looked at her and flashed her an evil grin followed by a wink.

"I can't do this," Gabriela whispered as she stood up.

"Gabi, you're not alone. He can't touch you. He's chained up." Seth reached for her hand and guided her back down to the seat. He gave her fingers a gentle squeeze as the judge took his seat.

"Okay, first on the docket is bail for Diego Montez…how do you plead?" asked the judge.

"Not guilty, Your Honor." Diego flashed a smile and looked over his shoulder again at where Gabriela sat with Justin and Seth.

"Your Honor, the defendant was caught literally in the act attempting to rape his niece. We request he be remanded. Her injuries were extensive, and an exam showed injuries sustained over years of abuse," said the district attorney.

"Your Honor, my client has a right to a speedy trial. My client requests his trial be today. He has a right to face his accuser."

The judge looked between both sides for a brief moment. "Trial will be set for today after lunch."

"But, Your Honor, that's not enough time to get witnesses here," complained the district attorney.

"Well, you better find a way then. This man has already sat in jail for a month. I will see you back after lunch."

Gabriela watched in horror as Diego grinned at her as he was led out of the courtroom by the bailiff. When Diego blew a kiss at her, she flew out of her seat and out of the courtroom in tears. She ignored Seth and Justin as she called out after her. She ran through the courtroom doors and down the stairs, straight into the chest of someone.

"Whoa, where's the fire?" said the stranger.

"I'm sorry," sobbed Gabriela, taking a step back. She looked up and took a step back in shock. The chest she bumped into was her uncle's lawyer.

"I'm glad you ran into me… I have some questions for you." He looked around to see if they were alone before speaking to her again. "Your uncle was right…you're a cute one," he said, reaching for her face. "Your uncle sends—"

"Hey!" shouted Justin as he rushed down the steps with Seth close behind. "Gabi, go stand with Seth," he ordered.

"Ah, Sir Justin, I presume?" The man smiled as his eyes followed Gabriela's every step.

Justin sniffed the air and gave the man a warning glare. "I know what you are. Stay away from her," he growled, allowing his eyes to flash black in color before returning to their normal color.

"I was simply trying to comfort her…she seemed distraught," he said, still staring at her.

"Seth, take Gabi back upstairs." Justin took a step to the side, blocking the man's view of Gabriela.

"You alphas, are so strict." The man chuckled. "I have to say, the young alpha's mate is quite beautiful and unmarked…" The evil grin that he flashed Justin made him growl.

"This is your only warning…if any more of your rogues are caught trespassing, they will be tortured and killed." He recognized the man's scent as one from the outside of the pack house.

"Tortured and killed for delivering a message? Alpha, how rude… I guess I should deliver it now.

Unless one of my soldiers already delivered it to you…"

"He didn't give us a message. He gave us a fucking riddle. What does it mean?"

"It means that your future luna was offered to us in a deal, and I don't appreciate your pack offering something and then changing their mind."

"No one would dare betray me and make a deal like that!" He growled and took a step toward the rogue.

"Well… I guess it sounds like you have a traitor on your paws." He stepped around Justin to head back up the stairs. "You will turn the human over to me before the end of trial, or the judge will do it for you."

Gabriela and Seth waited outside of the courtroom for Justin to return. She had managed to calm down and stop crying but was far from okay. Seth had her tucked under his arm protectively. The district attorney was waiting for them as soon as they came back up the stairs to let them know what to expect during the trial.

Dad, she's not doing so good. She shut down, he linked his father.

I'm on my way. Make sure her uncle's lawyer doesn't go near her, he responded. *He's on his way up the stairs. He's one of the rogues that was at the house. I recognize his scent.*

Right when Justin mind-linked that warning, the rogue came up the steps. Seth narrowed his eyes at him as he walked past them into a nearby room. "Gabi, we have a while before court…you should eat."

"I'm not hungry," she responded as she stared at a wall.

Seth sighed as he stood up. His dad had just come up the stairs with a worried look on his face. "We have to talk but not here." He gave Seth a warning look before glancing over at Gabriela. "Gabi… you really should eat."

Gabriela jumped out of her seat as the courtroom doors slammed open, banging against the walls. "Attention. The case of the *People versus Diego Montez* has been moved up. Court will be in session in five minutes," announced the bailiff before turning back to enter the room.

"No! They can't! My aunt's not here!" Gabriela shook her head sobbing. "This can't happen like this!"

Seth pulled her into a hug to try and comfort her. "Shhhhh, it will all be okay. It will—"

"No, it won't." She pulled out of the hug. "He got away with beating me for years. Every time someone would find out, someone would warn him that he was going to be investigated and that we had to move. This is him pulling strings! He's going to kill me this time!"

Seth felt the mix of anger and sorrow his wolf was generating. He could literally smell his mate's fear. "Kitten, you're not alone anymore. You have a family now…our family." He tilted her head up and wiped the tears from her face.

"And trust me, Gabi, my family is like a pack of wolves…we protect our own," said Justin with a smile. "Come on, let's head inside." He opened the door to the courtroom.

They filed into the pew a few rows behind the district attorney's table. Gabriela looked up in fear as her uncle was led back into the room, still in shackles. He shuffled over to the table where his lawyer was already waiting. She watched the two men whisper back and forth before they both turned to her and smiled.

"All rise," ordered the bailiff as the judge entered.

The judge sat down and addressed both sides of the courtroom before Diego's attorney started opening arguments followed by the district attorneys. Not long after, the district attorney began to call witnesses to the stand that were then questioned by Diego's lawyer.

Once Gabriela was called, she slowly made her way to the witness box. She answered each question that the district attorney asked her. She told the court how Diego had beaten her over the years and all the details that had led up to the day he tried to rape her.

"Thank you, Gabriela, your witness," he said to the defense as he took his seat.

Gabriela took a deep breath as the man approached her. "Gabriela, you told the court that your uncle abused you…correct?"

"Yes," she said, not daring to look at Diego.

"Yet you told no one about it…why?" He leaned on the wooden ledge of the witness box, winking at her. "If he beat you so badly, why would you keep quiet?"

"Because I was afraid. I get harsher punishments if we have to move." She looked down at her fingers. The look Diego's lawyer gave her made her uncomfortable.

"Let's talk about the day your uncle supposedly beat and tried to rape you…you said he hit you so hard you started to black out…correct?" He looked at her as she nodded. "You say you remember him tearing your clothes, but how would you know if you were blacking out?"

"I-I," she stuttered. "I was—"

"Isn't it true that you had to ask the doctor if you were raped?"

"Yes," she said quietly. "But—"

"Did your uncle rape you?"

"No, but—"

"No further questions. I'm done with this witness." He walked away from Gabriela who was sobbing in the witness box. "Oh, Your Honor…my client would like to amend this case to include custody of his niece. Her biological aunt failed to present herself today, leaving the minor witness abandoned.

"No!" she shouted. "You can't do that! I won't go with him…please! My aunt is letting me stay—"

"With a stranger who has not been vetted or approved to be a temporary foster parent," interrupted the lawyer.

"No…no! Please, don't" she begged, looking at the judge as the bailiff gently led her out of the witness box back to her seat.

Seth pulled her into him as he glared at her uncle. "Seth, I can't go back… I can't…" She buried her face into his chest as he rubbed her back. This wasn't at all how she imagined her day going. She knew it wasn't going to be easy, but she didn't imagine it would be this bad either.

The rest of the trial went by in a blur. Both sides gave their closing arguments and took their seats. "Mr. Montez, please rise," the judge ordered. "You waved your right to a jury trial…by doing so, you give this bench the authority to find you either guilty or innocent. I have found you guilty of the lesser charge of simple assault. You have no history of such acts in the past. I suggest it does not happen again. As for the charge of rape, I find you not guilty. I am sentencing you to time served." His gavel hit three times before he continued speaking. "As for the custody of your niece, I do find that your wife failed to appear and by doing so making you the only relative present. I order the minor, Gabriela Montez, into the custody of her uncle." He slammed the gavel one more time before rising to his feet with a sympathetic look on his face at Gabriela's reaction to his ruling.

"No…please, you can't do this…please!" She begged as she looked at him. "I can't go back…" She turned her head in panic to Justin. "Please, don't let them take me! Please…"

Justin looked at his son as he searched for what to say. He saw the look on the judge's face. It was a look of guilt. The whole trial was rigged.

"Gabi, let's go," came her uncle's voice from behind her, making her whole body go rigid. He reached for her arm, only to have it swatted away by Seth.

"She's not going," he growled.

"She is…the judge said so, now move away from her." He reached for her again, this time tightly gripping her arm. He pulled her away from him, ignoring her cries. "Now, this time, listen to my warning, boy. Stay away from her!" he hissed, dragging her away.

Justin put his arm on Seth's shoulder. He could feel his body shaking in anger. His eyes were black, and his nails were turning into claws. "Son, control him…we will figure this out." Justin pulled Seth in for a brief hug as Diego's lawyer approached them.

"Alphas, it was a pleasure doing business with you both. Our new luna will be well taken care of." He grinned. "Your pack member is quite the negotiator. Well, I have to go… I have a new luna to meet."

Chapter 13

Gabriela sat in the back of the expensive SUV between her uncle and his lawyer. She hadn't stopped crying since she was ripped away from Seth and dragged out of the courthouse.

"Gabi, that's enough! Stop crying!" ordered Diego.

"Please...let her cry...it's not every day that one meets their mate." Diego's lawyer ran a finger up Gabriela's arm. "My name is Max," he said, introducing himself to her.

"Speaking of mate, how will this work. You said that this will help keep me out of jail, right?" he asked Max, ignoring Gabriela's curious stare at him.

"It will...once you turn, the rules change." He lifted Gabriela's face to his so that he was looking directly in her eyes. "Do you know what a mate is?" he asked her. When she shook her head no, he chuckled. "Unmated...unmarked...and naive," he growled with lust. "We are almost home. I will explain what should have been explained to you a while ago." He grinned as the vehicle slowed to a stop in front of a huge house. He stepped out and waited for Diego and Gabriela to exit behind him. "Welcome to the Red Rogues."

Gabriela struggled against Diego's grip as he dragged her toward the door behind Max. Once inside, she looked around in shock and disgust. She could see past the foyer into a family room and dining room which was dark in color with dark furniture. The house stunk of smoke, alcohol, and sweat.

"What is this place?" she whispered to herself.

"This, my dear Luna, is your new home," said Max, ripping her from her uncle's grip. He pulled her through the house and out the back door.

She looked at him with confusion and fear. She had only heard the word *luna* once before, and that was from the two little kids she saved from being attacked at Seth and Justin's house. He snickered at the look on her face before tossing her to the ground outside, letting out the most inhuman howl she had ever heard.

"Do you know what I am, Gabriela?" he asked as he stalked toward her. He let out an evil laugh when she shook her head in fear. "Fine… I will show you." He took another step toward her when his bones began to crack. His spine began to bend while his face grew a snout, and he sprouted a tail.

Gabriela propelled herself backward from the horrific sight in front of her. Where Max once stood was now a large brown wolf with red eyes. She rolled over to her knees and sprung to her feet, running away from the massive wolf. She heard the wolf's growl close behind her as she neared a line of trees. As soon as she entered the woods, she saw a few more red eyes in the distance followed by growls and howling. Realizing how close they were, she bolted for the next tree and began to climb. She was shaking and out of breath by the time she made it to a height where she thought the wolves couldn't reach her. Gathering up her courage, she leaned over a little to see a group of wolves gathered below.

"Gabi! Isn't this great?" she heard her uncle from below. She peeked over again to see him coming up to the tree. "They're werewolves! We are going to be one of them!" he called to her. "Gabi, come down." He let out a groan of frustration. "I'm not going to ask again...get down here."

A few moments passed when Gabriela heard the same cracking she heard before. She watched Max change from a wolf back to a very naked man. "Gabriela... I don't have all day. Come down here before I go up there," he growled. The smile he had on his face earlier at the courthouse was replaced by an angry scowl. "I'm going to count to three. If I have to come up and get you...you will have more than just me to deal with." He punched the tree in frustration. "Fine, have it your way," he growled. "One...two...three, here I come." He let out an animalistic growl and reached for the tree.

"Wait… I'm coming down," she called. She slowly climbed down the tree, limb by limb until she made it to the bottom.

"Good girl," he cooed as he stroked her hair.

Gabriela closed her eyes and tried to lean away from his touch unsuccessfully.

"Come, we have a lot to talk about."

When Gabriela reluctantly stepped toward Max past her uncle, Diego grabbed her arm tightly, causing her to yelp in pain, which earned him a low growl from Max. Diego flinched back in fear, releasing her. "Diego…the first rule to learn about becoming a werewolf. We are territorial, which means *we don't share*."

Diego looked between Max and Gabriela before looking at the rest of the pack. "But you said that you guys share your—"

"Shut up!" he roared at him. "Rule number two. Obey the alpha and don't interrupt." He grabbed Gabriela and pulled her into him. "I said we share the lower-ranked females that don't have mates. You promised me anything I want in exchange for turning you into one of us…and I want your niece." He glared at Diego as he glared back at him, daring him to object to his terms.

When Diego did not respond, he pulled Gabriela the rest of the way to the house. She looked behind her at her unhappy uncle and the pack of wolves that followed close behind. "You see, Diego," he began as he pushed Gabriela down into a nearby chair. "You can agree to my terms and accept your niece as a trade for becoming one of us or… I can kill you and take her anyway. It's your choice."

Diego groaned. "I accept," he growled.

"Great. I'm glad you agree." He turned away from Diego to Gabriela. "Now that you know who and what I am…do you know what Justin, Seth, and the rest of the people they are always with are?"

Gabriela shook her head in denial. "You're lying…" she sobbed.

"I'm not, Little One." He kneeled down in front of her, ignoring the fact that he was still naked. "They are werewolves just like me, and you were Seth's mate…which would have made you their luna."

"Were?" she said quietly.

"One of Justin's pack members offered me an unmated, unmarked future luna…which means, Little One, you are mine. You *will* be *my* mate… *my* luna," he said with glowing red eyes. "But first, I have something I have to do. Don't run away this time… I won't be as nice if I have to chase you again," he warned.

He turned away from her and walked back over to Diego. "Red Rogues!" he announced. "I present to you, my chosen mate!" He pointed over to Gabriela as the wolves howled and barked in response. "And I present to you, the newest member of the pack." He turned to Diego. "I hope you survive the transition, my friend. You are the right kind of despicable." He grinned before shifting back into his wolf. He licked his snout before letting out an ear-shattering howl as the rest of the wolves howled in response.

Gabriela watched in fear as Max bit Diego's forearm, causing him to cry out in pain. As soon as he bit him, he released him, shifting back into his human form.

"Take him and prepare him for the transition," he ordered as the rest of the wolves began to shift into humans. He grabbed Gabriela and began dragging her into the house. "Now, let's get you settled in."

Chapter 14

Justin and Seth sat outside the courthouse, waiting for Justin's beta, Chris, to show up. Justin had a hunch that the trial was fixed somehow, and he was determined to figure out how. Seth was inconsolable earlier when they were forced to watch his mate being dragged from the courtroom. Just as Chris was pulling in with Jace in the passenger seat, Seth saw the judge from Diego's case exit the courthouse. Without warning, Seth took off after him.

"Seth!" shouted Justin as he raced after him. Justin didn't want Seth interacting with the judge until he had reinforcements to help keep him and his wolf under control. Wolves, especially alphas, are unpredictable when he, his pack, or his mate is threatened. "Seth! Don't!" he yelled.

"You! Do you know what you've done?" growled Seth. He caught the judge by the back of his neck and pushed him hard into the car face first. "Why would you rule like that? You saw the evidence. He was guilty!" He spun the judge around to face him.

"Seth! That's enough! Release him now!" ordered Justin.

"Not until he explains why he did what he did!"

"You're one of them," gasped the judge as he watched Seth's eyes turn black.

"One of who?" growled Seth, gripping the judge harder.

"Seth…let him go so he can tell us. Son, please…don't be like them," he pleaded. He placed a hand on Seth's shoulder. "I'm asking as your father, but don't make me ask as your alpha, son…please."

Seth allowed his wolf to let out a growl of anger before releasing the judge, allowing him to slide to the pavement. "He deserves to be treated how she's being treated right now," he said as he backed away. He moved so that he was standing in between Chris and Jace.

Justin kneeled down to the judge and held out his hand as an offer to help him up. When the judge did not move, Justin sighed. "I assume you know about our kind?" He waited for the judge to nod before continuing to speak. "I assume that Diego's lawyer told you about our kind?" The judge nodded again. "So I will ask you one time only, and I pray for your sake that you give me an honest answer because the young lady you sent away is my son's mate." Justin ignored Seth's growls behind him as he continued speaking to the judge. "Why did you rule in his favor? Everyone could see by the look on your face that you knew he was guilty."

"I had no choice...his lawyer, Max, came to me one day. He and some friends approached my daughter when we were out. They tried to kidnap her. When I told them I was a judge and I was going to have them thrown in jail, he said that he was going to make me a deal that I couldn't refuse." His shoulders sagged as he started to cry. "He said he would see me at home... I thought he was some crazy junkie, but he and his friends showed up as I was going out to pick up dinner. He was a man one minute then the next a wolf! Then he turned back again! He promised to leave my daughter alone if whenever he had a case in my courtroom, I ruled in his favor. Any criminal he wanted, they were to be released to him. Ever since then, he's been using my courtroom as a recruiting tool." He looked past Justin to Seth with tears in his eyes. "He said that he was going to take my daughter and breed her! Like she was livestock! I'm sorry, I'm so sorry." He brought his hands up to his face and sobbed.

"Breed her?" asked Chris. He and Jace grabbed Seth tightly. He barely had control over his wolf as it was, and with each word out of his mouth, they knew it was a matter of time before that control was gone. "What do you mean, breed her?"

The judge looked at Seth before looking at Justin. "I don't know...just that they would breed her with the others if I didn't comply. My daughter's human!"

"So is Gabi! You let her abusive uncle who tried to rape her walk away with her!" Seth pulled against Jace and Chris as he growled.

"Get him out of here!" ordered Justin.

He watched painfully as his son was dragged away. He understood Seth's pain. When Seth's mother was killed, he was inconsolable, and he didn't want for his son to suffer the same pain he went through. He pulled the judge up from the ground. "I understand you wanted to protect your daughter…but you condemned another girl to a life abuse and maybe even worse. If something happens to her, I won't be here to stop my son from coming after you. After I calm my son, I will be back here in two hours. You will give me every piece of information you have on Max and every person he represented here."

"You-you aren't going to kill me? Or t-t-take my daughter from me?"

"Not all werewolves are animals. Wolves, like Max, give the rest of us a bad name. All I want is my son's mate back…" He dusted off the judge's shirt and shoulders. "See you in two hours." Justin turned and walked away.

He wanted to hurry back to Seth. He needed to make sure that he was in his right mind so that they could figure out who the traitor was and where

Gabriela was so that they could get her back. Time was running out, and rogues were not known for being patient, and whatever they had planned for Gabriela would be happening soon.

Chapter 15

"Little One! Open the door! We will not be late to the ceremony," growled Max. He impatiently pounded on the bathroom door to the room he was keeping her locked in. "You can open it or I can break it... you have three seconds to decide."

Gabriela sighed from the other side of the door. "Please, I just want to go home," she sobbed.

"This is your home now. Get used to it, and open the damn door," roared Max. "Have it your way!"

When he didn't hear any movement from within the bathroom, he broke through the door and grabbed a frightened Gabriela by her arm, forcing her out of the bathroom. "You will learn to be obedient," he growled as he pulled her behind him. "When we get there, don't speak...do you understand?"

She nodded, keeping her gaze on the ground as she pulled at her clothes with her free hand. Max had forced her to change into a gown for some ceremony that he was having. She spent three days locked in her room while Max educated her on the werewolf world. Apparently, Max was a rogue that was in the process of creating his own pack. He had convinced other rogues to join him while turning humans into werewolves to serve under him. Today was the ceremony to accept Diego as a pack member and formally introduce Gabriela as his chosen mate. She learned that each wolf has a mate and that she was apparently Seth's.

"We're here. You stand by me the whole time," he ordered as he pulled her through the crowd of bodies close to a huge fire in an opening of a field. "Members... I called this ceremony to introduce and accept Diego Montez as a new member of the Red Rogues!" He smiled as the crowd of men howled and applauded. "Diego has offered his niece as my luna! I present to you, Gabriela!" He yanked her arm, pulling her closer to him. Ignoring Diego and Gabriela's glares, he let out a howl, causing the crowd to fall silent. "Today, they will accept the brand of the Red Rogues so that the world will know who they run with... Bring me the brand!"

Gabriela watched in horror as three large men pulled long sticks from the fire, exposing red hot tips on the ends with four connected double *R*s in cursive that connected at the top as if they were meant to mirror each other.

"No!" she shrieked as she pulled against Max.

Max chuckled as he pushed her toward two more men. "Little One, you don't have a choice." He grabbed the first poker and held it up. Two of the three brands were relatively small. "The luna carries two brands!" he announced as he closed the space between them. "The first represents the pack…" he said as he placed the hot iron on the inside of one of her wrists.

The men howled as she screamed in pain. "Stop! Please!" She cried out again as Max removed the poker from her skin. When he reached for the other one, she tried to pull away again. "Please, don't," she begged as the men twisted her other arm out, exposing the inside of her wrist.

"The second and last brand represents her mate." He grinned at Gabriela. "Little One, look at me," he ordered, with glowing red lust-filled eyes. "This second brand represents me. Your mate." He pressed the hot metal to her other wrist, ignoring her screams. After a few moments, he removed it and handed the brand back to one of the men. "Welcome to the Red Rogues, Little One," he said to her as he pulled her from the men. "You belong to me now."

He turned toward the crowd and howled. "Now, the next brand is for our newest member… Diego!" He turned to him with the hot poker in his hand. "Diego, by accepting my brand, you accept me as your alpha. You will follow any orders given to you.

You will protect this pack…and *my* luna," he said with a different tone as he stepped in front of him, interrupting his lustful gaze he had on Gabriela. "Do you accept?"

"Yes, Alpha," he responded.

Max could sense the detest in his tone. "Then repeat after me, I, Diego, accept you, Max, as my alpha and my niece, Gabriela, as your mate and luna."

Diego's gaze settled on Gabriela who was shaking her head, pleading with him silently not to agree. "I, Diego, accept you, Max, as my alpha and my niece, Gabriela, as your mate and luna." He looked at Max as he placed the hot poker on his bicep, hissing at the pain. His human side wanted to say no to Max and claim her as his own like he always wanted, but his wolf overpowered him.

"Welcome to the pack, brother," said Max. "Red Rogues…let's party!" He howled before pulling Gabriela close to him. "Little One, I present you to our pack." He gestured toward all the men who were standing off to one side as a group of women were being led toward them by another group of men.

She let out a whimper as they stepped into the dim light from the fire. The women that they brought out looked to be a little older than she was with cuts and bruises everywhere that they were not clothed. They were barefoot, and their clothes were torn and barely covered them. "Little One, meet the women of the pack. They are responsible for keeping our men happy, fed, and producing pups for our pack..."

Gabriela's eyes settled on their stomachs where she could see that some were indeed pregnant. "Are they...human?" she asked softly as a tear escaped her eye.

"Most of them, yes," he responded as he leaned into her, inhaling the smell of her hair. "We breed them as humans at first...once they begin to show signs of weakness or sickness...we turn them so that they can continue to produce. If a wolf chooses one for his mate after they have contributed enough pups to the pack, then they may be released from their producing responsibilities...but that rarely happens. Rogue wolves rarely settle down unless it benefits them."

"You're monsters...all of you," she whispered in disgust. "You're treating them like cattle."

"Yes, we are monsters." He chuckled. "But you're wrong about one thing...cattle are slaughtered when they can't produce. Think of this as a puppy mill...everyone gets re-homed." All the men broke out in laughter at Max's comment. "So accept it, Little One, because now that you've been formally introduced, I will mark you...and mate you."

She pulled against him again unsuccessfully. "B-but you just...you already marked me," she cried. "W-why do want to b-burn me again?" She looked around as everyone laughed around her.

"Oh, my Little One, you are so naive. I have no intentions of burning you again," he said with a grin. He pulled her into a hug and rested his face in her neck with his lips lingering in between where her shoulder and neck met. "My intentions are to bite you here..." he growled as he kissed her before pulling away. "That will let any wolf know who you belong to. Once I mark you, we will mate...then you will rule my pack with me as my luna."

"No! I won't let you!" she screamed, repeating his words. "I will never want to be with you! You're disgusting!" She spat at him. "You're worse than my uncle! I hate you!"

Max let out a threatening growl before grabbing her forcefully and throwing her with so much force she landed close to the crowd. "You *will* learn to mind your manners and your mouth, Little One," he warned. "And you *will* not disrespect me as your mate and your alpha!" He walked over to her and grabbed her by her throat, lifting her off the ground. "And let me be the first to tell you that you are wrong," he snickered, releasing the grip from her neck. He chuckled as she crumbled to the ground, coughing as she gasped for air. "Once you're in heat...you will be begging for me."

Chapter 16

Jessica

Jessica stood outside the pack house with the other members of the pack. It's been a week since the little human was awarded to her uncle, and she was confused as to why Alpha Justin and Seth would ask for the whole pack to gather for an announcement. She was hoping it was to announce her as the pack's replacement luna. Since Gabriela disappeared, she took over the responsibilities that Gabriela would have been responsible for if she would've been formally introduced to and accepted by the pack. She'd been unsuccessfully attempting to comfort Seth since his mate vanished after they left the court-house. When he and Justin returned without her, Seth locked himself in Gabriela's room, refusing to come out even when she went to visit him to assure him that she was there if he needed anything. She looked around at the rest of her pack members when she noticed the two little kids that Gabriela defended during the attack. She plastered a fake smile on her face as she walked toward the kids. She despised little kids but needed to make a good impression if she wanted to be Seth's chosen mate and the pack's replacement luna.

"Hi, guys," she said. "How are you doing today?" She kneeled down next to the kids.

The kids smiled at her. "Good," said Jack. Jack stood up and handed Jessica a dandelion.

"Oh…a weed, thank you." She grimaced as she accepted it.

"It's not a weed, it's a flower," he said with a proud smile.

"Can we have ice cream?" asked Jackie.

Jessica shook her head. "No, the ice cream is for big pack members…grown-ups. I'm sure you understand," she said as she stood up.

"But Luna Gabi gave us ice cream," whined Jackie.

"Awww, but Luna Gabi's not here," she said, not bothering to hide the agitation in her voice.

"Is Luna Gabi okay? Momma said that she was taken away," said Jack as he pouted.

"I'm sure wherever she is, she is keeping busy." She grinned as she turned away from the kids to head back to the spot where she was standing previously.

"I miss Luna Gabi," she heard Jackie say, causing her wolf to growl.

She rolled her eyes as she walked away from them. She reached her spot just as Justin and Seth emerged from the house, followed by Jace and Chris. She smiled to herself as all four of them stood on the raised porch. Seeing Seth out of Gabriela's room with a determined look on his face made Jessica assume he was ready to make the announcement she'd been waiting for since she had her first shift. She looked around at everyone around her and smiled.

"As you know, Seth found his mate recently," began Justin. "A badly treated human that attended the same school as some of you." He looked around and cleared his throat. "Your future luna was legally awarded to her abusive uncle by a judge who was being blackmailed by one of the rogues that attacked our pack!"

Gasps and whispers of panic began to erupt from the crowd.

"Your future luna proved to me, my dad, and all of you that she didn't need to be a wolf to defend this pack." Seth's eyes connected with Jessica's for a brief moment before he continued to look around at everyone else before speaking again. "She ran toward a rogue and defended two pups that were in danger even after being warned to stay put…to stay safe… Gabi, being a human, ran toward danger with nothing but a bat." His voice broke, causing him to stop talking.

"The rogue that helped her uncle said that someone from this pack…my pack made a deal with him for Gabi," growled Justin, causing the crowd to bow their heads in submission and fear. "That rogue says that there is a traitor among us…and I'm sure that the traitor that made that deal is the same one who gave him the information about Seth finding his mate, information about where our borders aren't patrolled, and directions to the pack house!" he roared. "This is a warning to the traitor and to the whole pack…when I find out who the traitor is, you will regret your decision. Your decision to betray not only me but this pack…your friends and family that you put in danger." There was a scary calmness in Justin's voice.

Jessica's smile faded instantly at his words. This wasn't the announcement she was expecting at all. She tried not to panic as she felt a pit of fear grow in her stomach when Seth stepped back up next to his father. Max assured her that there was no way that they would link her to the judge. The judge knew what she looked like because she was the one to approach Max and give him and the judge all the details needed to throw the case. It was supposed to be a simple grab and go…not a failed kidnapping and an attempted murder of two of her younger pack members. Max promised her that once he marked and mated Gabriela, he would approach Justin and request an alliance since in the werewolf world, a minor human can't be mated without parental or guardian permission. That would force Seth to let her go along with any hope of her returning back to him. She needed to contact Max and make sure that she was marked and mated soon.

"If anything…" Seth paused. He remembered how bad of shape she was in when they took her in. He cleared his throat to continue, "Everything that happens to Gabi while she's missing will be held against those found guilty of assisting those mutts!" he growled. His dad put a hand on his shoulder as his phone rang.

He used his wolf's hearing to listen to Justin's call with the judge, but so did Jessica. They listened as the judge told Justin all the information of each case that Max told him to fix along with descriptions of the individuals who came with Max to set up Diego's case in order to be awarded custody of Gabriela.

"Great, we will see you in a couple hours," said Justin to the judge before hanging up the phone. "Everyone is dismissed," said Justin.

Jessica watched as Justin, Seth, Chris, and Jace walked into the house. She hurried away from the others toward her car as she pulled out her cell to text Max. "We have a problem," she texted. "They linked you to the judge, and they're going to meet with him! He's going to give them a description of everyone who was with you for that human and her uncle's case!" She sent the text as she slid into the driver's side. She waited a few seconds to see if Max responded. Even though she was given strict instructions to not contact him and to avoid the territory that they recently claimed so that Justin and Seth never made the connection, she was panicked enough to go by if he didn't respond by the time that she made it to town.

"I will take care of the judge. Meet me in an hour in my territory in my office. Make sure you're not followed." Jessica read Max's response. She checked her watch before checking her phone again. Max's territory is a long way from her own pack. She started the car and threw it into drive as her wolf whined to her. She could sense that her wolf was afraid and embarrassed at Jessica's actions to try and be luna of the pack. Her willingness to do anything to get what she wanted might just get her expelled from her pack or worse.

Chapter 17

Max dragged Gabriela out of her room down the hall. "This is your home now! This is your life!" he growled at her. "The sooner you accept that, the better." He opened the door to his office, dragging her in. "We are going to have company. Are you going to be a good little luna and behave yourself, or do I have to restrain you again?"

Gabriela pulled against him unsuccessfully. "I hate you," she spat.

"I guess that's a no." He yanked her toward his desk and pulled out one of the chains connected to the corner of his desk. He cuffed the shackle around her neck. "Sit," he commanded as she yanked at the chain. She glared at him before taking a seat in the chair next to his. "Now, when our visitor gets here…don't speak." He put a finger under her chin, forcing her to look at him. "You keep your eyes on the floor." Gabriela opened her mouth to respond, but a knock at the door interrupted her. "Enter!" he shouted without breaking eye contact with her.

"You said this plan was foolproof! First, you fail at the pack house, and then your stupid rogues almost kill two pups from my pack!" shouted the familiar voice.

Gabriela broke her gaze with Max to see who the voice belonged to.

"You said it would take them months to figure out that it was an inside job!" shrieked Jessica.

"Jessica?" said Gabriela in shock. "You did this? You helped them?" She stood up as Max grabbed her arm painfully. "Why? I did nothing to you!" she cried.

"Gabriela," warned Max.

"Nothing?" she yelled back at Gabriela. "You ruined everything! I was supposed to be Seth's mate! I was supposed to be luna! Not you!" she yelled. "You're nothing but a weak, pathetic, helpless human!" she spat.

"Watch your tone, pup!" growled Max at Jessica. "You would do well to remember that this is not your pack. Speak like that again to her and you won't have to worry about them finding out it was you," he warned. "And if you ever yell at me again, I will make you wish they kill you before I'm done with you. You might get away with talking like that to your Alpha and his pup, but you won't get away with it here. You won't get another warning."

Jessica bowed her head in submission. "With all due respect," she said through gritted teeth, "the judge has my description. Seth will know who he's talking about when they get there."

"The judge won't be giving anyone's description," he said as he settled in the chair next to Gabriela. "He lost his ability to speak. I need to make sure I have enough time to train my Little One," he said with a smile as he looked at his chosen mate.

Jessica nodded, ignoring his fixated gaze on Gabriela. "Are you still planning to offer the alliance?" she asked.

"My intentions have not changed, pup. You kept your end of the deal, I will honor mine," he said to Jessica.

Jessica leaned over to the side to get a better view at Gabriela. "I see she's not marked yet," she commented with disgust.

"Watch your tone."

"I meant no disrespect…it's just that Seth has no intentions of giving up on her. He's not going to move on as long as she's…*available*."

"Let me make myself clear… I will mark her when I want, how I want, and where I want." His eyes were glowing red out of anger and annoyance that she had the nerve to question him and use an annoyed tone at the end of her sentence. "I will send word to your Alpha within the week. Don't contact me again." He waited to see if Jessica responded before standing up. "Oh, and, pup?" he called to her to get her attention. "Disobey my orders again about reaching out to me and you will join as one of the women of my pack…the men in my pack are always looking for new fun…my pack always can use new breeders."

Jessica's eyes darted to Gabriela who was glaring at her with tears freely flowing from her eyes. She unsuccessfully tried to ignore the pain and hurt that was evident in Gabriela's eyes. She glanced at the shackle around her neck along with the cuts and bruises that littered her body. A small pit of guilt formed as Max's words registered in her mind. She wanted to be Seth's chosen mate and the pack's luna, but hearing about how the women of Max's pack are treated and seeing how he treated his own chosen mate felt like she made a mistake. The harshness of his words and actions made her realize that Max didn't care if Seth or Justin figured out it was her that gave him the information. He only took care of the judge because he needed more time for his plan with Gabriela. Jessica was a tool just like the judge. Max probably killed him right after he got what he wanted.

She bowed her head in acknowledgment. "I understand," she responded.

"Good. Now, I have a lesson to teach my mate about obedience…before you leave, you should take a look at your future as a reminder." Max stood up, dragging Gabriela by her chain. He unhooked the bottom connected to his desk, ignoring Jessica's uncomfortable look.

"Thank you for seeing me, but I really have to get going. I have—"

"Enough!" he roared as he stalked toward Jessica, dragging Gabriela with him. Jessica shuffled back away from him until her back hit the wall. "You don't disobey me, disrespect me, or my mate… human or not!" he growled. "You need to see what waits for you if you mess up again, pup!" He threw the door open and dragged Gabriela out of the office. "Follow me!" He yanked the chain, ignoring Gabriela as she tumbled down the last few steps in the stairwell. Jessica followed behind with her head down. "I need straps!" he yelled as he walked out of the back of the house.

Instantly, two wolves appeared with leather straps and a whip. Gabriela and Jessica watched in horror as the wolves hooked the leather straps to two posts already standing in the yard. "No! Please!" cried Gabriela. "Don't do this! Jessica, don't let them do this!" she pleaded as Max dragged her to the posts.

"Ha, ha, ha, you think she's going to help you?" he said as he tied her arms to each post. He pulled the straps tight so that her arms were spread straight out. "She's the one who set you up!" He chuckled as one of the wolves handed him the whip. "Are you paying attention, pup?" He laughed as he cracked the whip before bringing it down across her back.

"You were told to behave!" *Crack.* "To be submissive!" *Crack.* "Not to speak!" *Crack.* "You." *Crack* "Are." *Crack.* "Mine." *Crack.* "So you better start acting like it," he growled as her body sagged, leaving her hanging from her restraints, her legs no longer supported her. He turned to face Jessica, whose face showed nothing but fear.

"You see what happened to my chosen mate, pup? Imagine how our pack women are treated." He pulled Jessica's head back by her hair. "I trust you found your lesson helpful?"

"Y-yes," she said as she watched Gabriela's limp body being released from the straps. The blood trickled down her back and legs. "I-I u-unders-stand."

"Good. Leave and *never come back*." He watched as Jessica backed away, slowly looking back and forth between Gabriela's bloodied body and Max. As soon as she was a few yards away, she turned and bolted for her car.

Max chuckled as he turned toward Gabriela. "Have the she-wolves take her to her room. Make sure they chain her before they treat her."

The wolves nodded as Max leaned into Gabriela's nearly unconscious body. "Remember, Little One, you brought this on yourself." He waved off the wolves to take Gabriela to her room. "Now... Red Rogues! Time to train! We have a meeting to crash!"

Chapter 18

"It's been almost two weeks, Dad! Who does he think he is to set up this meeting? He stole my mate!" screamed Seth as he paced the floor in Gabriela's room. "I can't just sit here waiting for him to bring her here! Only goddess knows what they've done to her!"

"Seth, we have no choice. Our only lead we had disappeared when the judge died. Max will be here tomorrow, and his messenger said that Gabi would be with him. I've called a pack meeting tonight with the pack warriors and trackers." He held his arm out for his son. "Everyone's waiting outside for us. Let's go."

Seth stood up and followed his father out of Gabriela's room. They quickly made their way down the stairs and out of the house. He followed his dad to the patio where Chris and Jace were already waiting.

"Alpha, everyone you requested is here. No one has been briefed," said Chris as he bowed.

"Thank you, Chris." He took a step forward. "You are here because you are my best warriors… my best trackers. The rogue that has Gabriela has created his own pack and is requesting an audience to negotiate peace with our pack. Gabriela is our luna. She belongs here." Just as he took another step forward to continue his speech, he heard the sliding glass door open.

Seth turned to see who came out to interrupt the meeting. He rolled his eyes as Jessica stepped out with a pitcher of sweet tea and a plate of cookies.

"Sorry, Alpha, no one told me that there was a meeting," she said as she bowed to Justin. "If I would've known, I would've had everything set up."

Seth rolled his eyes again. "No one told you, Jessica, because no one wanted you to know," he growled at her.

"Seth, she is only trying to—"

"I don't care what she's trying to do, Dad! She has no business here or anywhere else that she's been showing up!" yelled Seth, interrupting Chris.

Jessica bowed her head in submission at Seth's outburst. When he let out a feral growl, she flinched.

"Jessica, you—" began Justin before a number of howls sounded somewhere in the distance. Justin growled as another howl sounded closer to the house.

"Dad," said Seth as a large gray-and-brown wolf with red eyes stepped around the corner.

A few moments later, Max appeared in human form, dragging a dazed, barefoot Gabriela close behind as the pack warriors and trackers moved out of the way of their future luna and her captors.

"Gabi!" he yelled in excitement. He tried to run toward her, but his dad, Chris, and Jace grabbed him when both the large wolf and Max growled in protest. "Get off me!" he growled.

"Alpha Justin, Young Alpha," said Max as he bowed, ignoring Seth. "Forgive our unannounced arrival. I know our meeting was for tomorrow, but I was just too excited to wait."

Seth growled out again. "Kitten, look at me," he pleaded. "Gabi?"

"Oh, Young Alpha, I apologize for her rude behavior. Say hello, Little One," he ordered.

Gabriela's gaze never left the ground as she responded. "Hello, Alphas," she said softly.

*Seth, calm down…*ordered Justin through the link.

Dad, can't you see there's something wrong with her? She's under some kind of control!

I will have her aunt brought out here to help snap her out of it, but we need to appear civil for this to work, ordered Justin through the mind link. *He's using her to get to you.*

Justin cleared his throat. "Thank you for bringing my son's mate back to us. That will help with our peace negotiations," said Justin. He sent a message to Jack and Jackie's mother to bring Gabriela's aunt out through the mind link. He's been having the kids, their mother, and Gabriela's aunt staying in the pack house to try and help keep Seth calm until they came up with a plan.

Max chuckled as he pulled Gabriela into his body, causing a growl to erupt from Seth. "Alpha, it is still wolf tradition for human minors to be given away by a family member, is it not?" he asked Justin mockingly. When Seth growled again, he smiled. "It's been so long since I've been in a pack, I wasn't sure." He ran his fingers through Gabriela's hair as she kept her eyes on the ground.

"What's your point, Rogue?" spat Justin.

"My point, dear Alpha, is that this Little One has already been offered as a human mate to a pack…to an alpha as a chosen mate. You see, I am no longer a rogue." He flashed a wicked grin at Justin before looking at Seth. "You know what, Little One, I think it's warm enough that you can take your sweater off."

"Yes, Alpha," she responded quietly as she shed her long sweater, leaving her in a short halter top and a pair of short jean shorts.

"There you go, Little One." Seth glared at Max as he taunted him, staring at Gabriela with hungry eyes. "Have a seat, Little One, remember your form."

"Yes, Alpha." She slowly sunk to the ground in front of Max, crossing her legs, leaving her arms and back exposed to Justin, Seth, Chris, Jace, and Jessica.

"Oh my goddess," gasped Jessica in shock. She brought her hand to her mouth at the sight of the scars on Gabriela's back.

"What. Did. You. Do. To. Her," growled Seth.

"Relax, Young Alpha, I am here to make peace... with my chosen mate." He motioned to Gabriela who still sat on the ground in front of him.

"Have you lost your damn mind?" shouted Justin as he grabbed Seth again to try and keep him in place.

"Of course not, Alpha... Gabriela was offered to me. I asked her uncle for his permission to make her my mate, and he agreed." He locked eyes with Seth before continuing to speak. "Of course, she needed some training...she was very disobedient, weren't you, Little One?"

"Yes, Alpha."

"I've had enough of this, Dad... Gabi!" Seth struggled to free himself from everyone's grip. He broke eye contact with Max and looked at his mate's badly scarred back. "Kitten...what did he do to you?" he said quietly to himself.

"Young Alpha," he chuckled, "she did this to herself," said Max without emotion.

Seth's eyes turned black, and his claws began to emerge as he slowly lost control of his wolf.

"She wouldn't have received lashes of disobedience if she behaved herself. Stand up," he ordered.

Gabriela complied. "Yes Alpha," she said as she stood up facing Max for a moment before he turned her to face the pack house.

"So, Alpha, are we going to discuss peace or not? I feel a lot of hostility here." He pulled Gabriela into a hug, burying his face in the crook of her neck as he locked eyes with Seth before locking eyes with Justin and back to Seth again. "I put off marking my mate for this alliance," he said as he dragged his canines across her neck where a mark from her mate would go. "If there is no deal to be made…" Max retracted his canines just as the sliding glass door opened.

"Oh my god, Gabi!" Karina bolted out of the house but froze when her eyes landed on her battered body. "Gabi…" she sobbed.

"She won't answer you…any of you. She can't. Your Gabriela is gone." Max chuckled. "I did you all a favor by bringing her here before I mark and mate her."

"Gabi!" screamed Karina. "I know you're in there," she pleaded as Gabriela's gaze remained on the ground.

"Luna Gabi!" shouted two little voices from the doorway.

"Kids, go back inside!" Jessica shouted angrily. Max's sudden appearance worried her that he was here for an ulterior motive than originally discussed when he approached her looking to take Gabriela as his mate.

"Luna Gabi!" they shouted again. Gabriela's slowly raised her head at the sound of their excited voices, snapping her out of her daze.

"You came back!" said Jackie. "I told you she would come back!"

Her eyes darted back and forth between the faces before her as if she had just arrived and was seeing them for the first time. Her eyes locked with Seth's as a small sob escaped her. "Seth…" she whispered softly.

Max growled, yanking her head back by her hair. "Tsk, tsk, Little One… I said complete silence and obedience," he growled louder, allowing his claws to emerge on his free hand, using it to grip her shoulder, drawing blood.

As she whimpered in pain, both Seth and Justin howled in unison, causing howls to erupt all over. The pack warriors and trackers that stood nearby growled as they bared their teeth at Max and the wolf in front of him. The wolves closed in around Max, Gabriela, and the other wolf, closing off any possible routes of escape.

Max looked around as his eyes began to flash with a red glow. "Alpha, control your pack," he growled. "You wouldn't want word to get out that you lured a newly formed pack to your territory under false pretenses." He dug his claws deeper into

Gabriela's arm as a visual warning, causing everyone to growl louder. "We wouldn't want anyone getting hurt…again. Besides, your new luna said that our deal would be honored. After all, I'm only taking what is rightfully mine since you killed my mate, Alpha." He flashed an evil grin at Jessica.

"What? No… I—" she looked around frantically. Her heart sank as growling faces turned from Max. This probably was his plan all along. He never mentioned Alpha Justin killing his mate when he approached her. "It's a trick! He's just—"

"No need to hide it, pup. We all do what's necessary to protect our pack." Without warning, Max yanked Gabriela by her arm behind the wolf that he brought with him. Wolves lunged from all directions as red eyed wolves approached from the sides.

Chapter 19

"It's a trap!" yelled Seth as he jumped down and took off after Max with Justin close behind.

Justin and Seth caught up to Max a short distance from the pack house where another large red-eyed wolf stood, who shifted into his human form.

"Diego," growled Seth at Gabriela's uncle whose human form replaced the large wolf that was there not long ago.

"End of the line, Max. You are done here. You attacked my pack and stole my son's mate. Give up," spat Justin.

Max yanked Gabriela in front of him, pulling her back close to his chest. "That's where you're wrong, Alpha... I'm not done until I say I'm done." He harshly pulled Gabriela's head back exposing her neck and shoulder. "My mate was pregnant with my pup," he cried in agony. "You took everything from me! Years ago, you killed a she-wolf on your lands after a rogue attack...*my* she-wolf...*my* mate," he growled. "You took my mate and my pup from me!"

Justin's eyes turned black with rage. He knew what Max was talking about. The she-wolf he was talking about had killed Seth's mother, who was Justin's mate, in a rogue attack when Seth was only five years old. "Your mate died because she attacked my pack! My mate! An attack that you ordered! You killed her yourself as soon as you ordered her to step foot on my land and attack us!" spat Justin.

"You know, Alpha…as you know, the loss of your mate drives you mad, but the loss of a child kills you inside." Max erected his canines and lowered his head to Gabriela's neck. "You will see how that feels when you watch your son wither away to nothing!" He bit into Gabriela's neck as he made eye contact with Seth and Justin, forcing her to scream in agony as he forcefully marked her.

"Nooooooo!" screamed Seth as he watched him retract his canines and lick the blood around Gabriela's mark with glowing eyes.

"Like I said, she is my chosen mate. She belongs to me…she's mine! And after I kill you both, I get to keep her and your pack!" He grabbed hold of Gabriela tightly and threw her into a nearby tree, knocking her unconscious just before lunging at Justin as Diego lunged for Seth.

Everyone clashed at each other, throwing blow after blow before shifting into their wolf forms, clawing and biting each other's fur. After what seemed like hours of fighting, Seth and Justin slowly began to gain the upper hand, drawing blood from their opponents. As Seth's jaws snapped at Diego's throat, Justin managed to pin Max on his back. He bit at his throat hard enough to cause Max to start to bleed out but not hard enough to kill him instantly. He shifted back to his human form as Max whimpered in pain.

"Shift," ordered Justin.

Max growled as he allowed his body to change.

"Link the rest of your pack and call them off!"

Max grinned as he coughed up blood. He looked over and watched just as Seth bit down on Diego's shoulder. Seth viciously shook his head side to side, causing Diego to howl in pain. As Seth tried to adjust himself to bite down again, Diego managed to pull free. Max's grin disappeared as he watched Diego's wolf abandon the fight and retreat into the night.

"Call them off!" he ordered again with a growl.

Max turned his gaze to Gabriela who was still unconscious on the ground near the tree. "She will always be hunted," he said, coughing. "She will always be a target." He coughed up more blood as it became harder for him to breathe. "She will never trust werewolves." He looked at Seth and grinned as his breathing became labored and less regular. "She will never trust you," he painfully coughed out.

Justin placed his hand on Seth's shoulder as they watched Max exhale his last breath. "He's gone, son, it's over." He bent down to check Max's pulse quickly as Seth rushed over to Gabriela.

"Gabi? Gabi, Kitten, can you hear me?" Seth asked as he gathered her limp body in his arms. He adjusted her head as she spoke again. "Gabi, please wake up!" he cried. "I'm so sorry this happened to you." He sobbed as blood flowed freely from her body. He rocked her back and forth as he silently prayed for her to wake up.

"Seth, we have to get her back to the doctor," Justin said softly.

Seth nodded and stood up, cradling her closely to his chest. He took off running back toward the pack house, not bothering to wait for his father. Justin as Alpha had to bring Max's body back to the rest of the pack as confirmation of his kill. Seth ran for what seemed like an eternity as he cleared the tree line near the house.

"Kara! Kara!" he screamed. He stepped over the bodies of dead wolves that littered the ground.

Kara ran out of the house, intercepting Seth at the stairs to the patio. "Take her to the infirmary," she ordered. She took off after Seth as he rushed Gabriela toward the pack's medical ward. They barged through the double doors and down the hall toward the emergency wing. "Put her on the bed." Seth complied with Kara's instructions. "Dear goddess, what happened?" she asked as she started an IV in her arm.

"Not now…just…just save her, please…" Seth wiped the dirt and blood from her face as Kara pulled out a syringe. "What's that for?" he asked as he watched her load the needle.

"Her injuries are extensive. She'll need stitches for starters. I need to make sure she stays sedated until my exams are complete," she responded as she slowly injected the clear liquid.

Once the syringe was empty, she scanned Gabriela for open wounds. She quickly stitched the gash on her hairline from hitting the tree and the wounds on the front and back of her right shoulder from Max's claws. Her eyes settled a bit above the claw marks where Max's mark was. She quickly averted her eyes to continue her exam. She slowly ran her fingers down her arms, pressing on her muscles but paused when she reached the burn scars from the brands on her wrists. She looked up at Seth's teary eyes. "Maybe you should wait outside while I finish the exam. I know this is hard for you."

He shook his head in response. "No, I can't be away from her. Ever. Again."

Kara slowly nodded as he struggled to keep control of his wolf. She could see how much it hurt him to see his mate in such bad shape. After a few hours of tediously reviewing Gabriela's body, Kara had stitched the bottom of her feet, her hairline, behind her ear, her shoulder, her arm, and forearm. The x-rays taken after her open wounds on her back from a recent whipping were treated showed a few rib fractures and a punctured lung that was partially collapsed.

"You can come in now," said Kara after she finished covering Gabriela up with a blanket. Justin had stopped by to check on her condition but had him and Seth step out so that she could change her into a medical gown.

Seth and Justin shuffled in the room with worried looks on their faces. They each pulled up a chair as they looked at Kara expectantly. "How long will she be out for?" Seth asked.

"If I don't medicate her again, she will be under until tomorrow morning," she responded before excusing herself from the room.

Seth looked at his dad before looking at his mate. "How did this happen, Dad? How did they get close enough to do this?"

Justin raked his hand through his hair. "I'm so sorry, son," he began. "We never expected for humans and werewolves who aren't mates to work together against us," he confessed. "It's the one thing we never planned for." He cringed as he waited for Seth to ask the million-dollar question.

"What happened, Dad? How did you miss that he was the rogue that killed Mom?"

"Seth...it's not as simple as it sounds—"

"Why not, Dad? I know I was only five when it happened, but people's looks don't change that much. Especially if they're a wolf!"

"Because I never saw his human form! They attacked us as wolves, not humans. I never knew what he looked like until the day in the courtroom. Even then, I didn't know it was him until he told me."

"But still, why would he do this to her if he hated you for what happened? She had nothing to do with it!"

"Because in his mind, I didn't just kill his mate… I killed his pup when his mate died. He wanted a pup for a pup, and his only way of getting even was killing you slowly by taking Gabi."

Seth shook his head in disbelief. "Look at her, Dad," he said, nearly in tears. "He beat her, he whipped her…he marked her!" he growled through gritted teeth. "He's right! After this, she will never accept me as her mate! Thanks to him, she will be afraid of me…our kind did this to her," he said sadly.

"Max is not our kind," Justin said sternly to Seth. "Gabi's already seen the difference between us and Max," he said sadly to his son. "She's a smart girl. It might take some time, but you have nothing to worry about," he assured him.

"That's the problem, Dad, I have everything to worry about. Diego got away! He's still out there, and what about Jessica?"

"They're a problem for another day. I've already sent Chris and Jace to have Jessica present herself for questioning tomorrow, and the trackers are already looking for Diego and anyone else who was able to escape."

"I can't be present to question her. If she's guilty, I won't be able to control my wolf and keep myself from killing her…" admitted Seth.

"I wouldn't expect you to be there anyway. You need to be with your mate."

"Alphas?" came Kara's voice from outside the door before she entered. "I took the liberty of contacting Chris to request clothes be sent over from the pack house." She handed a bag to Seth and another to Justin. "He had some omegas pack some clothes and toiletries so that you can bathe here just in case you plan on staying."

"Thank you, Kara." Justin opened his bag as he stood up.

"There's a shower in the bathroom right over there, and there's another out in the hall. Dinner will be up shortly." She bowed quickly and exited the room, leaving the two alone again.

"Why don't you shower first?" suggested Justin.

Seth grabbed the bag and slipped into the bathroom. Not wanting to be away from Gabriela for too long, he scrubbed quickly before drying off and throwing on a pair of sweatpants and a plain white shirt. As soon as he exited, his dad headed for the bathroom just as Kara rolled in cart with a few different food assortments. He nodded in appreciation as she dropped off the cart with a smile. As soon as she left, he climbed into the bed next to Gabriela. Careful to avoid her injured ribs, he placed one hand across her stomach to hug her gently as he placed his other arm behind his head. He kissed her gently on her cheek before closing his eyes as he listened to the soft beats of her heart and the steady beeps of the machine monitoring her.

"Good night, Kitten, I'm so sorry I failed you… but I promise to spend the rest of my life making it up to you," he said quietly before drifting off to sleep.

Chapter 20

Gabriela slowly blinked her eyes open from the annoying beeping sound that lured her from her sleep. She held her breath as she felt the weight of an arm across her stomach. She could hear the machines beeping increase as her heart rate sped up.

The intensified beeping snapped Seth awake almost immediately. "Gabi," he said softly. "Gabi, you're okay now. You're safe." He pushed himself up on his elbow and reached to tuck her hair behind her ear, causing her to flinch as if she had just been burned.

"N-no, d-don't!" she shrieked as she backed away from Seth. She pressed herself against the bed rail before pushing herself over the railing, landing with a thud on the tile floor.

"Gabi, you're safe...please, calm down," he pleaded with her as he climbed off the bed after her. As he took a step in her direction, she let out stifled cry.

"S-stay away!" She scooted herself back into a wall, yanking her IV out of her arm. "P-please...d-don't," she sobbed.

"Gabi, it's me, Seth. I would never hurt you." He frowned at his scared mate. "Kitten, please, don't be afraid of me," he begged. Realizing that he was getting nowhere with her, he slowly reached for the call button near the bed. A few moments later, Karina ran through the door, followed by Justin and Kara.

"Gabi!" said Karina. "Honey, what happened? What are you doing down there?" she asked softly. She looked at Seth who hadn't moved an inch since he pressed the call button. "Sweetie, you need to get back in bed." She took a step toward her niece but paused when Gabriela squealed in fear. "Honey, I know you're afraid. You've been through a lot, but you have to let us help you."

"N-no," she stammered. "M-Max...h-he... you..." she stuttered out, pointing at Seth and then to Justin

"Goddess, she's having a panic attack," said Kara as she neared Karina's side. "She needs to calm down or she'll have to be sedated."

"Kitten, Max can't hurt you anymore," said Seth. He looked at his dad who had a sympathetic look on his face. *She's afraid of us,* he linked to Justin.

I know she is... Max gave her a reason to fear us, he responded through the link.

But we never hurt her! We would never hurt her!

I know that, Seth, but she doesn't. We have no idea what Max told her or what he did to her. You have to be patient. She's been through a lot, especially for a human.

Seth nodded at Justin. "Kitten, I know you're afraid, but I need you to breathe. Look at your aunt." He took a slow step to the side as Gabriela locked eyes with Karina.

Without breaking eye contact, Karina slowly made her way to Gabriela, pulling her into a hug. "It's okay, I got you." After a few moments of sitting with her on the floor, Karina cleared her throat. "Gabi, you need to get back in the bed." Motioning toward Seth, she leaned toward her niece. "I know you're afraid, but Seth is going to help get you back in the bed, okay?" When Gabriela began to panic again, she put her hands on Gabriela's face. "He's not going to hurt you, I promise...okay?" Gabriela nodded slowly as Seth approached them. "Just keep looking at me, I promise everything will be okay."

Gabriela flinched slightly as Seth scooped her up from the floor and placed gently her on the bed.

"Th-thanks," she whispered as he pulled the sheet over her. Seth nodded and gave her a small smile before taking a step back. After a few moments of her aunt coaxing her to let Kara restart an IV since she managed to rip hers out from scrambling out of bed, she leaned back on the pillows, careful not to look Seth or Justin in the eyes.

"Gabi, I'm sure you must have some questions you want answered," said Justin.

"No, Alpha," she said just above a whisper, lowering her gaze to the floor.

"Gabi, call me Justin. You knowing my pack status doesn't change anything between us…okay?"

Gabriela nodded, maintaining her gaze on the floor.

"Kitten, you don't have to be afraid to look at us. We would never hurt you. You know that, right?"

When Gabriela didn't answer, Justin gave a small smile before raising a finger to Seth. "Gabi… I know you're afraid of us because of Max." Justin paused when he saw her flinch at the sound of his name. "But you need to know that he doesn't represent what we are…or who we are." Justin took a step toward her bed and kneeled so that he could see her eyes. When she went to look away, he leaned over to an angle to see her eyes again. "Gabi, look at me," he instructed softly.

"Look at us," added Seth, kneeling down by his dad. She slowly raised her head so that she could meet their stares. "See? It's still us…just no secrets this time."

"Let us answer your questions, okay? Anything you want," said Justin with a comforting smile.

When she nodded, both he and Seth let out simultaneous sighs of relief. "What's your first question?"

Gabriela gulped down the lump in her throat. She had so many questions to ask but wasn't sure what question would offend or upset them. After a few moments of internal debates with herself, she took a deep breath. Out of all the questions running through her mind, there was one that needed to be number one. "How long do I have until I change? Until I become…like him?" she asked sadly as her hand found its way to the bite mark on her neck.

Seth cringed. Of all the questions she could have asked, he hated that this had to be the first one. "You don't have to worry. The bite he gave you won't turn you…he marked you," he said sadly.

"But he bit my uncle, now he's a werewolf too."

Justin ran his hands through his hair. Having to explain a mating bite to a human was hard, but explaining the difference between a mate's bite and a conversion bite was going to be a nightmare. "Gabi, when werewolves have a mate, we mark our mates here," said Justin pointing to his own neck. "Claiming them as ours to protect, to love…to cherish. Then our mate would do the same to us and mark us back." Gabriela's fingers danced along the edges of the gauze that covered Max's mark. "Werewolves are given a mate, a soul mate by the moon goddess. Our mate is our other half, almost like how humans are when they get married but more intense."

Gabriela shook her head at Justin. "But Max beat me!" she screamed. "He branded me, then strung me up and whipped me!" She held her wrists out at Justin. "He wasn't protective, cherishing, or loving," she cried out.

Justin nodded his head at her so that she knew he understood how she felt. "Because he wasn't your mate," he told her. "No respectable werewolf would treat anyone that way…especially not their mate. Mates are a special thing, Gabi."

"I guess I'm not special enough," she responded.

"That's not true," interrupted Seth. "You are special, Kitten. You're so special it hurts."

Gabriela chuckled at Seth's words. "Yeah right, Seth. What would you know? According to Jessica, I'm just a worthless human who was worth nothing until Max—"

"Don't you dare finish that sentence, Kitten," growled Seth, causing her to flinch slightly. Seth's eyes soften at her reaction. "Gabi…just don't say stuff like that about yourself. Please."

"Why not? How do you know what she said isn't true?" she questioned him.

"Because you're my mate," he breathed, taking her by surprise. "Gabi, you're my other half."

"But… I'm not a werewolf, I'm human."

Justin smiled at Seth's confession to his mate. "I'm going to leave you two to talk." He rose to his feet, shooting a warm smile to Gabriela. "Take it easy. I'll be back to check on you later," he said to her before letting himself out.

Once they were alone, they sat in a comfortable silence with each other for a while. Gabriela, who was still reeling from Seth's confession, drew invisible lines on her hospital blanket. She was actively trying to think of what to say, but it was Seth who broke the silence.

"Kitten, it doesn't matter if you're human. What matters is that you're my mate…and that I'm yours." He slowly slid toward her and reached for her fingers. "Do you feel the tingles? The sparks?" he asked as he slowly laced their fingers together. "That's proof that we're made for each other." He smiled when she didn't flinch or pull away from his touch. "Gabi, please, let me show you how you should've been treated from the beginning…show you that not all wolves are monsters," he begged.

She took a deep breath as she stared at their interlaced fingers. As much as she tried to ignore them, the sparks were there, and she couldn't think of anything to explain them away.

"You don't have to make your decision now," he assured her. "How about this, get to know us…get to know me. The real me, Gabi. The pack already loves you. Especially after you took on a wolf with only a baseball bat to defend two kids you didn't know," he said with a laugh. "And Jack and Jackie have been begging to see you."

She smiled at the thought of the two little ones. "Okay…fine," she said softly.

"Really?" He didn't bother to try and hide the excitement on his face.

She giggled at his reaction. "Yes, really."

"Thank you! I promise you won't be disappointed." He beamed at her as he pulled out his phone. "Now…there are two little pups outside with your aunt driving her crazy to come see you."

Chapter 21

"Luna, can you please read for me?" asked a little voice to Gabriela as she nodded in response to the pup.

Seth watched from the doorway as Gabriela sat on the floor of the orphanage that was just recently opened after her discharge from the pack hospital. Max's attack had left a lot of pups without parents, and when Gabriela found out, she insisted that there be an orphanage built.

"Okay, everyone, gather around... Zoe asked me to read her a book." She smiled at Seth as Zoe plopped down on Gabriela's lap. "I think it's only fair that if I read a book, I get to have ice cream... but if everyone listens, we all get to have ice cream!" The kids squealed in excitement as they sat down and listened to the story from the book that Zoe had picked.

"How's she doing?" asked Justin quietly to Seth as he walked in the door.

"Really good actually," he responded. "As much as she denies that she should be the luna, she's acting like it more and more every day. The kids love her."

"Everyone does." Justin leaned back against the wall and listened to Gabriela as she continued to read the children's book to the pups. He was hoping to talk to both Seth and Gabriela about her formally accepting her position as Seth's mate and the pack luna now that she had found something that she enjoyed. Gabriela stepping up for the pups of the pack was another act of kindness that she showed, making the pack embrace her even more...human or not.

"The end," she said to the kids, bringing Justin out from his thoughts. "Okay, everyone, grab your jackets and head over to the pack house. Make sure you tell Karina you listened to the story and earned your ice cream!"

"But you have to come with us, please, Luna Gabi?" pleaded Zoe as tugged on her hand.

"I will join you guys later but first, Alpha Justin looks like he has some questions about the story."

Zoe nodded before running out the door. "You are really good with them," said Justin as he and Seth followed her out of the orphanage.

"Thanks..." she grabbed her bag and headed toward the pack house.

"Gabi, please...you can't avoid us forever." Seth jogged to catch up to her.

"I'm not avoiding you, guys, I'm just… I don't know." She turned to face them. "I know what you want to ask me, and I know it's already been almost two weeks, but I'm not who you're looking for…" She turned to look Seth in the eyes before continuing. "I'm just a girl, the wrong girl."

"Everyone here loves you and has already accepted you as part of the pack. That proves something," Justin countered.

She shook her head as she looked at Seth who only smiled at her. "Why are you smiling?"

"Because Dad's right. You say that you're not cut out for it, but you're doing exactly what a luna does. You've been doing it since you got here."

"Look, I'm not saying you have to make a choice now, but I would like for you to at least meet everyone…formally. When I introduce Seth as the soon-to-be alpha, if it will make you feel better, I won't introduce you as the future pack luna. Just meet everyone," he pleaded.

"I guess I can do that," she responded as she peeled her jacket off before fanning herself.

"Great, I can have Karina bring you some dresses out," Justin said to her.

"Great," she said. She pulled her sweater from over her head, leaving her in her cami aside from her jeans.

"Kitten, are you okay?" Seth asked.

Gabriela hated showing her scars, and she was doing that by stripping her clothes off on a chilly day.

"Yeah, I just-I don't feel good. I think I have a fever. It's hot." She wiped the sweat from her brow before turning toward the house. "I think I need to lay down."

"Kitten, wait." Seth reached for her shoulder as she started to stumble away. "Kitten, you're burning up!" He rushed around her and picked her up so that her head rested on his chest. "Dad, something's wrong. Humans shouldn't have a fever this high!"

"Seth, calm down. It's normal."

"How is this normal? Call Kara. I'll get her to her room. She—"

"Seth, stop. She's in heat."

"That's impossible. She can't be—" Seth paused as his dad's words sunk in. Only marked females who were virgins went into heat.

"Get her home. It won't be long before the fever turns into pain."

That was all Seth needed to hear from his dad. He took off toward the pack house as he held Gabriela close to his chest. "Hold on, Kitten. Hold on."

Chapter 22

"It hurts! Make it stop!" Gabriela was curled into a ball on her bed as Kara packed up her medical bag. "Please!"

"Gabi, I will be right back." Kara stood up and handed Karina an ice pack. "Try and keep her calm," she said to Karina before stepping out of the room.

"Alpha, you were right. She's in heat."

"Okay, so how do we stop it?" asked Seth. "She can't stay like this."

"Young Alpha, the heat will subside once she mates."

"I can't do that to her. Not this way." He shook his head as Gabriela let out another ear-piercing scream. "She needs to be in her right mind to make that decision."

"I understand, but your options are limited. The only other option is to re-mark her. I don't know how well that will work on her since she is human, but it works on the other she-wolves when they aren't ready for the mating process yet."

"But what if that doesn't work?" he asked.

"How about you go see, Gabi," recommended Justin.

Seth nodded as he walked into Gabriela's room.

"Seth, her fever is getting worse. Kara gave her a shot of something, but it's not helping," Karina said as she wiped Gabriela's sweaty forehead.

"I know," he whispered. "Kitten?" He slowly sat on the bed next to Gabriela. "Gabi?" he said as he laid down next to her.

"Seth…it hurts so bad… I can't…" she sobbed out as Karina reached for her.

"I know it does, Kitten." he looked up at Karina's worried face. "Karina, I need to talk to Gabi."

Karina nodded as she stood up. Once she was out of the room, Seth took a deep breath. Just as he opened his mouth to speak, she let out another scream that was louder than the previous one.

"Make it stop! Please, make it stop! It hurts!" she cried as she clutched her stomach.

"Kitten, I can make the pain go away," he whispered as he stroked her cheek.

"Please, do it…" she pleaded.

"Let me tell you what—"

"Just do it, please," she begged as he pulled her into a hug. "Just make it stop…make it go away."

"Okay," he whispered as he kissed her forehead. She let out a whimper as his kiss went from her forehead to her neck. When his lips reached Max's mark, he paused. "Kitten, I don't want to do this…not like this." He sighed as he kissed over Max's mark.

"Seth, please—" she began before letting out another scream

"Gabi, I'd have to mark you…" he said almost in a growl as he tried to keep control of his wolf. He wanted to give her every opportunity to change her mind, but more importantly, a choice to accept or decline to be marked…something that Max denied her.

"Just do it," she cried. "I trust you," she whimpered as she clutched his shirt.

"Okay, Kitten, I'm going to make it go away." He kissed her mark again as his canines began to grow. "I'm going to make it stop now…the pain's going to go away." His eyes were now black as he pressed one final kiss to her neck before biting down over Max's mark, pulling her close. He felt Gabriela's body begin to cool down almost instantly as her cries quickly changed from cries of pain to cries of pleasure. As soon as he retracted his canines, he licked the wound, sealing the mark.

"Seth," she whispered softly as he stroked the top of her head, "thank you." She nuzzled as deep as she could into Seth's chest.

"Shhhh, Kitten. It's okay now, it's over. I got you." He softly placed a kiss on the top of her head. "Good night," he murmured in her hair as he let his eyes close.

"Kitten, it doesn't matter if you're human. What matters is that you're my mate…and that I'm yours." He slowly slid toward her and reached for her fingers. *"Do you feel the tingles? The sparks?"* he asked as he slowly laced their fingers together. *"That's proof that we're made for each other."* He smiled when she didn't flinch or pull away from his touch. *"Gabi, please let me show you how you should've been treated from the beginning…show you that not all wolves are monsters,"* he begged.

She took a deep breath as she stared at their interlaced fingers. As much as she tried to ignore them, the sparks were there, and she couldn't think of anything to explain them away.

"You don't have to make your decision now," he assured her. *"How about this, get to know us…get to know me. The real me, Gabi. The pack already loves you. Especially after you took on a wolf with only a baseball bat to defend two kids you didn't know."*

Gabriela's eyes slowly opened from Seth stroking her arm, pulling her from her dream. "Good morning, Kitten. How are you feeling?"

Gabriela wriggled a little in Seth's embrace before answering. "Better," she whispered. "Thank you for making it stop." She nuzzled into his chest as he continued to draw circles on her skin. "I'm sorry about how I acted."

"Kitten, you don't have anything to apologize for," he said.

"Yes, I do. I've been unfair to you and Justin… and everyone here when you guys have been nothing but nice to me since the day I got here." She pulled out of Seth's arms and sat up.

"Kitten, everyone understands. You've had a lot to deal with." He sat up next to her.

"What happened to me?" she asked. "How did you make the pain stop?"

Seth let out a sigh as he raked his hand through his hair. "Kitten, promise not to freak out okay?" When she nodded, he gave her a soft smile. "Do you remember the mark Max gave you?"

Gabriela reached for the brand on her wrist.

"Not that mark, the other one."

She reached up to touch her neck.

"When a wolf bites its mate there, it kind of sets off an internal mating clock in a female. In your case, Max set off yours when he marked you. You went into heat."

"That's impossible, Seth. I'm human. Humans don't go into heat."

"Unless a human is marked by a werewolf. Then your body reacts the same as it would if you were one of us." He reached for her hand and interlaced their fingers. "Kitten, you need to know that in order for me to stop the pain… I had to mark you. I'm sorry, I didn't want to have to. Especially since Max—"

"It's okay," she whispered, looking at him. "You wouldn't have done it unless you had to. I trust you."

Seth smiled at her words. "You have no idea how happy I am to hear you say that."

She rested her head on his shoulder. "Now that you marked me, what does that mean?"

"It means that my mark replaced Max's, but unfortunately, you will go into heat again."

Gabriela frowned. "So it's not really stopped? It just got pushed back? I thought when you said you could make it go away, it would be permanent."

Seth coughed as he thought of a response to her statement. "Well, Kitten, I couldn't make it permanently go away."

"Why not?" she asked as Seth stood up from the bed and threw his shirt over his head, following him.

"Because Kitten, I-I couldn't. It wouldn't have been right for me to…"

"Why?" She stepped in front of Seth's path. "Seth, what aren't you telling me?"

When he realized that she wasn't going to let it go, he groaned. "Because, Gabi, you're a virgin."

"What does that have to do with anything?" she squealed. "And how do you know—"

"Because only unmated females go into heat. Unmated means virgins. You have to lose your virginity to permanently stop going into heat."

"Wait, what? We have to have sex?" She took a step back from Seth.

"No, we don't…unless you wanted to, but that's a choice that is yours to make and yours alone. No one else's. That's why I marked you instead, and I didn't even want to do that without consulting you first, but..." he sighed. "Kitten, all people have done to you your entire life is take away your ability to make your own choices. I couldn't take that choice from you."

Gabriela nodded slowly as she looked in his eyes. "So now what?" she asked nervously.

"Now, we do whatever you want."

Chapter 23

"I present to you, my son and future alpha, Seth, and Gabriela!" Justin smiled as Seth walked into the pack hall with Gabriela by his side, keeping their fingers interlaced. They made their way up to the stage as the audience applauded. "Many of you have known him since he was just a pup, but I am proud to say he will make a great alpha when it's his time to take over the pack."

Seth grinned as he squeezed Gabriela's hand. "Thank you, Dad...thank you, everyone, for coming to the presentation ceremony. Gabi and I appreciate your support. I know I have big shoes to fill." He laughed. He looked at his mate who nervously smiled as she looked around. "Relax, you're making me nervous," he told her.

"Very funny, Seth." She playfully smacked his arm as he guided her through the crowd behind Justin.

Making their way to their table at the front of the room, the rest of the room followed suit and made their way to their tables. Gabriela smiled as she took her place next to Seth and Karina, who was standing next to Justin. Karina and Justin had become quite close since their move into the pack.

"Karina, would you like some wine?" asked Justin as he pulled her seat out for her.

She shook her head no as she leaned toward Gabriela. "I'm so happy you decided to give him a chance," she whispered to her.

"He did save my life, more than once. I owe it to him." Gabriela took a sip of her water. "Hey, Seth?" she asked as he scrolled through his phone. "What's the status on...*her*?" Justin had purposely postponed the introduction ceremony twice with the hope of locating and questioning Jessica but had no such luck. "It's been a month."

"Kitten, we're still looking." He flashed her an apologetic smile as he reached for her hand. "She'll turn up. Don't worry." The truth was he was beyond worried that she hadn't been located yet, and it bothered him that Gabriela was worried about her still missing. He shot his dad a cautious look as Gabriela relaxed back into her seat.

"Gabi, I was wondering. How would you like to start back to school?" Justin took a sip of his wine as Gabriela's face lit up.

"Really? I can go back?" she squealed. "Yes!"

Seth glared daggers at his father who ignored him as he continued his conversation. "Of course, there will be steps you have to follow for security reasons."

She nodded. "When can I start?"

"It depends on a few things. We can discuss them after the ceremony."

Gabriela nodded at Justin as she squeezed Seth's arm. She had been switched to homeschooling for quite some time and desperately wanted to get out of the pack house. Seeing Seth's unhappy face, she frowned. "You don't want me to go back, do you?" When he didn't respond, she sighed. "I can't stay locked up forever, Seth."

"Kitten, I'm not saying you need to be locked up, I'm only saying until everyone who helped Max is taken care of…you shouldn't leave the house."

"Seth, that's enough. We can discuss this after the ceremony." Justin glared at Seth before turning his attention to Karina, who was playing with the napkin on the table. Just as the servers began to bring out the food, he smiled at Karina. "I haven't had a chance to thank you for helping me with my pack." He raked his hand through his hair nervously. He had come to adore Karina. Since her arrival, she had been nothing but supportive of him and his pack while keeping a watchful eye over Gabriela. The pack not only accepted Karina as the future luna's aunt but as a member of the pack.

"You don't need to thank me. I'm happy to help."

Seth chuckled. "I know you are, but I have to tell you, most humans are not this receptive to my kind."

Karina reached for Justin's hand. "Most humans haven't looked deep enough," she said softly as she stared into his eyes.

Justin smiled, losing himself in Karina's big brown eyes. "Let's get this party started. I think we have some things to discuss." He patted Karina's hand as he took a deep breath. Even though his mate, Seth's mother, was his true mate...the pull he was feeling toward Karina was so strong that his wolf was stirring deep within. It was a feeling he hadn't felt in quite some time. Feeling how giddy his wolf was, he knew that he would have a question to ask Karina after the ceremony...if she would be his mate.

Chapter 24

"What do you mean he's dead?" growled Jessica at Diego.

Once Justin ordered her to present for questioning, she left the pack, stating she was going to run some errands and disappeared for almost a month before escaping to the Red Rogue's territory.

"I mean I watched your alpha kill him!"

"This is all wrong! Goddess, what have I done? Now I can't go back!" she sobbed. "It wasn't supposed to be like this! This wasn't the plan! I was supposed to be Seth's luna, not that human!" she spat angrily.

"Who cares? You wanted to be a luna, just be one here. It's still a pack." Diego sat in Max's and spun around in his leather chair. "It can't be that hard, can it?"

She growled at him. "You don't understand. This isn't my pack. I don't belong here! I'm supposed to be with Seth, not here with...you." She paced the floor as she tried to think of ways to fix her current situation.

"Listen, little girl, this wasn't my plan either, but here we are. Obviously, you can't go back, so tell me, what do we do? I'm new at this wolf thing, and I want what's mine," he growled. "It seems that your old pack has things that we both want."

Jessica stopped pacing the floor to look at Diego. "What are you talking about?"

"I'm talking about you wanting to be with that annoying little brat that couldn't mind his own business and the brat has my niece." He grinned and leaned forward on the desk.

"With Max dead, there will need to be a new alpha." She walked over to the window where she watched the she-wolves tending to the wounded Red Rogue warriors.

"Fine, I'll do it."

"Ha! You?" She laughed as she scrunched her nose up at his assumption. "You can't be the alpha."

"Why not?" he asked in an agitated tone.

"Because you don't know the hierarchy…or the rules," she spat. She walked over to the desk where Diego sat. "If Max has a beta, that will be the next alpha." She smiled as a thought crossed her mind. Even though Diego wasn't familiar with the werewolf world yet, he was on the right track. "And the next alpha surely would want revenge for the killing of the previous alpha." She squealed in excitement as she rushed out of the office and through the house. Once she made it outside where the pack was, she cleared her throat. "Red Rogues…many of you recognize me as the one who made the deal with Max for your luna that was taken by your alpha's killer."

"Why are you here? You don't belong here!" yelled a voice from the pack.

"You're right. I don't belong here, I belong there with my pack, but your luna is with my alpha," Jessica growled. "My offer still stands. Your pack is welcome to the little human… I just need to see if the new alpha of the Red Rogues will agree." She took a step back and looked at the faces in front of her to see if anyone would step forward. After a few moments, a growl erupted not too far from where she was standing.

"I was Max's beta," said a tall form making his way toward her. He growled at her before stepping to the side and looking at the pack members. "As Max's second-in-command, I assert my right as the next alpha of this pack. Anyone who wishes to challenge me, speak now." He paced back and forth as he waited for someone to speak up. When no one spoke, he howled. "I, Lucas, claim the Red Rogue pack as my own! I am the alpha! Red Rogues, submit!"

Lucas looked around as every pack member bowed their heads in submission to him. Once he was satisfied, he turned toward Jessica. "Now, you said you had an offer?" He raised his eyebrows at her as his eyes raked over her body. "I need a luna, and you look like you would do fine," he said as he licked his lips.

Jessica rolled her eyes. "I'm not interested, but… I do have an offer," she said with a grin. "The intended luna of your pack." She turned toward the house and began to walk, swaying her hips side to side, beckoning Lucas to follow.

"I'm listening." He followed Jessica into the house and up to Max's office. Watching her perch herself on the desk, he plopped down in the chair and leaned into her.

"You as the alpha get everything that belonged to Max…that includes Gabriela," she purred.

Lucas grinned. "But she's not here…and you are. Why not stay here and be my luna?" he asked her.

Jessica rolled her eyes again. "I am here to offer you the same deal that I offered Max. Gabriela as luna of the Red Rogues. He had her, but he couldn't keep her. He let his anger get him killed. I need her gone from my pack so that I can be luna." She crossed her arms and narrowed her eyes at him. "Do we have a deal?"

Lucas nodded his head. "Yeah, we have a deal. But let me be clear." He stood up, towering over her. "My terms won't be the same as his. I don't care who dies from your pack. If you want to make this deal, understand that I will take what I want, and I don't care what I have to do to get it," he growled out.

Jessica shrunk back at the change in Lucas's demeanor. She was hoping that Lucas wouldn't be as bad as Max was, but his response to her offer made him seem worse. Determined to not make the same mistake twice, she cleared her throat. "What do you mean?" she asked innocently.

"I mean that Max was stupid to try and hold a meeting with the pack that his stolen mate came from," he growled. "I mean I will accept your offer since you are eager to get rid of her and since she was chosen as the luna to this pack, but don't expect meetings, alliances, or any stupid shit like that. And Max tolerated your disrespectful behavior… I won't. So, little traitor, are you sure you want to make this deal?"

Suddenly unsure of her decision, she slid off the desk and away from Lucas. "What if I don't want to make the deal?" she said quietly.

"Easy, then we make a new deal." He walked over to Jessica with an evil grin on his face. "You see, traitor, here it's an eye for an eye. Here, when you offer something…you deliver. You offered us a luna, twice now…and she's not here. Either we make the deal and we get Gabriela permanently, or you can take her place." He ran a finger down Jessica's cheek, causing an involuntary shudder of disgust. "I'm sure you saw Max's little lesson, right?"

Jessica nodded as she recalled Max having Gabriela strung up and whipped. She let out a shaky breath as she readied herself to voice her decision. "We have a deal," she responded.

Chapter 25

"I still don't agree with this," grumbled Seth as they pulled into the school parking lot. Today was the day that Gabriela was returning to school against his judgment. "You could finish the rest of the semester out at the pack house...where it's safe."

"Seth, your dad said that I can come back. I can't hide at home forever." She got out of the car, leaving Seth fuming inside.

"It's not hiding, Kitten. It's being smart." He hurried behind Gabriela and rushed to cut her path off before reaching the school steps. "Gabi, there's been no sign of her anywhere."

"That's a good thing, right?" she said as she tried to step around him unsuccessfully.

"Wrong, Gabi. It's a bad thing. Real bad." He placed his hands on both of her shoulders, forcing her to meet his stare. "Jessica isn't sophisticated enough to just disappear the way she did. That means that there's someone else helping her."

Gabriela's shoulders sagged at Seth's confession. "But she was the one helping Max...and he's dead."

Her eyes darted around the parking lot before she looked back at Seth. "Do you think my uncle...?"

He shook his head. "No. No offense, but your uncle isn't smart enough to help her disappear the way she did. He's a new wolf. He would need resources...new wolves don't have those."

Gabriela frowned. "This can't be happening... I can't—"

"Shhh, Kitten, calm down. Look. How about we go inside and see how your first day goes." He took her hand and guided her toward the school. "Most of the staff here are pack members, so if you don't feel comfortable, we can just go home."

She nodded as she followed him through the doors. She took in the sight of the long hallway as they made their way to her locker. She smiled softly. "God, I can't believe how we met." She chuckled, remembering back to Seth's attempt to get her to talk to him.

"Me either," he growled as his memories of her injuries flooded his thoughts.

Sensing the anger in his voice, she reached out for his arm. "Seth, don't be upset." Her words were soft and calming.

"It shouldn't have gotten—"

"Seth, stop," she breathed. "You can't keep blaming yourself for everything." She buried her face in his chest. "Promise me you will stop."

"Kitten—"

"Promise me," she said in a stronger tone.

"Listen to my little Luna giving orders...so demanding," he teased as he buried his face in her neck. "I promise."

"Good...and I'm not your luna. Let's get to class."

"Not yet you're not, but you will be," he said as they headed into class.

*****

"God, I can't believe I actually wanted to come back here." Gabriela packed her things into her book bag from her locker.

"You didn't like it?" asked Seth.

"Class was fine..." her voice trailed off as they walked outside.

"So what's wrong?"

"Everyone was staring...and bowing!"

"What's wrong with that? You're their—"

"Don't you dare say it, Seth. I'm not. They shouldn't be bowing to a human. I should be bowing to them!" She slid into the passenger side of the car.

"Gabi," he sighed as he started the car. "Please stop putting yourself down because you are human."

He hated that her being human was the one negative thing that stuck with her, thanks to Max and Jessica. Even though Gabriela came to trust him, his dad, and the pack, she let the fact of her being human be the deciding factor that she shouldn't be luna of the pack. Even though she won't admit it, her being a human leader among wolves scares her.

Deciding not to continue the conversation, he flipped on the radio so that they could drive home in silence. The drive home was brief. Seth parked the car in front of the house before turning to Gabriela.

"Gabi, look… I know you still are sorting out your thoughts. Just, please, stop letting their words dictate your decision." He reached across and squeezed her hand. "You are—"

"A weak, pathetic human who has been beaten and tortured her entire life! Don't you get it? How am I supposed to be your mate and lead by your side when I couldn't even save myself from Diego?" she cried before getting out of the car, slamming the door behind her.

"Kitten, wait!" yelled Seth as he chased her toward the house. "Gabi!" he roared, forcing her to stop in her tracks. He made his way toward her as pack members began to shuffle out from their homes from the loudness of Seth's voice. Ignoring the gathering crowd, he stood in front of her. "You keep using the fact that you're human as something to be held against you!"

"Isn't it?" she shot back.

"Gabi, no one here cares if you're human or not. All everyone here cares about is you! Not what you are! Don't you get it? They love you for who you are…because you're human! I love you because you are!"

"That makes no sense! Don't they understand I can't protect them? How can they expect someone like me to help lead and protect them?" she asked angrily, trying to fight the tears that threatened to fall.

"The same way you did when we were first attacked. Kitten, you took on a grown rogue wolf with two broken arms and a bat for two kids you didn't know. You ran toward the danger, knowing that you could get hurt. That's what a luna does, she protects her pack at all costs," he said softly to her. "You didn't know we were werewolves then, and on more than one occasion, you showed no fear in front of wolves…it didn't matter then, so why does it matter now?" he asked as he cupped her chin. "The only thing that changed since then and now is that you know about our kind…"

"And I, for one, am grateful that it didn't matter to you," came Kristen's voice from behind them. Gabriela turned to see Kristen clutching Jackie and Jack's hands, as she bowed her head to her.

"Please… Kristen, don't bow—" began Gabriela.

"You saved my kids. You didn't care who they were, but you went anyway. The young alpha is right. Actions are what define a true luna."

Gabriela gasped as more members from the pack stood behind Kristen, bowing their heads in submission to her. "Kitten, the whole pack was there that day," said Seth, linking their hands together.

"And they witnessed your bravery," said Justin as he exited the house with Karina close behind. "Gabi, you not only took on a rouge, you tried to take on the whole pack. When they tried to run to their mother, you still stood there, defending them as their protector."

Gabriela smirked. "Only because I didn't know she was their mom." She smiled at Kristen who smiled back.

"That's the point. That's *our* point...and not just me or the young alpha...that's the whole pack's point. You didn't know. You thought we were actual wolves," responded Kristen. "You took it upon yourself to protect them at any cost. Any werewolf will tell you that only parents and lunas defend children like that, and that is enough proof for us...all of us."

Gabriela stared in awe at all the faces that stared at her with admiration and support. The very reason she said that she couldn't be their luna was exactly why everyone was saying she should be. Realizing that everyone was waiting for her to say something, she gave Seth's hand a tight squeeze before clearing her throat.

"Thank you...thank you all," she said as she looked around at everyone. "You all have proven to me how wrong I was. I'm so sorry for how I've acted toward everyone." She turned to Seth before continuing, "You're right, I was letting what happened with Max and Jessica influence my decision... I'm sorry," she said to him before looking around at everyone. "I want you all to know how sorry I am... and yes," she turned back to Seth again, "I will be your luna."

Chapter 26

"I wish your mother was here to see this. You look beautiful," said Karina as she finished Gabriela's makeup.

It has been exactly six months since Gabriela agreed to be the luna in front of the whole pack.

"Your mom would be so proud of you."

She stood up and moved behind her so that Gabriela could see herself in the mirror. Tonight was the night of the acceptance ceremony for the pack for both Karina and Gabriela. Justin asked Karina to be his mate and current luna of the pack until Seth and Gabriela were ready to take over. Gabriela unconsciously smoothed out the imaginary wrinkles on her long-sleeved white gown, with a single sapphire lace wrapped around the waist with a sapphire diamond on the front. Karina gathered the bottom of her own gown, which mirrored Gabriela's dress in every way except for the color and headed toward the bed. Karina's gown was a sapphire blue, with a single white lace and a white diamond around the waist.

"I'm nervous," whispered Gabriela as she walked toward the bed. She quietly took the earrings and necklace that was left out for her and put them on. Taking a deep breath, she nodded at her reflection before turning toward her aunt. "I guess it's time."

"It is," she responded.

They both exited the room and made their way through the house and out the back door where a white path made of cloth was laid out lit by torches. They walked silently together down the path until they came to an opening where the pack stood waiting. Justin followed by Seth stood at the end of the white runner with huge smiles on their faces.

"You both look beautiful," said Justin as he reached for Karina's hand.

"Speak for yourself, Dad, Gabi looks gorgeous." He laughed as he took Gabriela's.

The two alphas walked the rest of the short distance up to the raised platform with their mates at their sides. After climbing the steps, they stood in the middle of the platform for a moment under the full moon, bathing in its bright light. After a few moments of silence, Justin stepped up, clearing his throat.

"I, Justin, alpha of the Black Paw Pack, have called this ceremony to bring not one but two new members into our pack. You all know that Seth and I have found our mates and lunas to this pack." He motioned for Karina, Seth, and Gabriela to step up next to him before continuing to speak. "I present to you, Karina. My chosen mate and luna of the Black Paw Pack!" He smiled as the pack cheered and howled at the announcement. After a few moments, he began to speak again. "And I present to you, Gabriela, Seth's mate and future luna!" The pack erupted in cheers again. "We all know that it's been a trying time for our newest pack members, but it's shown us how resilient we all can be. Tonight, under the blessing of the moon and our goddess, let us welcome them into our pack as one of us!" Both Seth and Justin took rings from their pockets and placed them on Gabriela and Karina's fingers.

Gabriela smiled as Seth led her down the stairs to the platform behind Justin as she admired her white gold diamond and sapphire swirl ring. Without warning, everyone began stripping their clothes off, causing her to hide her face under her hands.

"Seth!" she shrieked.

"Kitten, it's fine. You don't have to hide your face. I'm only—"

"Getting naked. Everyone is…"

"Yes, because we are going to run as a pack. Once we shift, you climb on my back, and we go for a run." He stroked the small portion of exposed skin not hidden by her fingers before stepping back from her to shift.

Gabriela waited until the sound of bones cracking stopped before removing her hands from her face. She reached out and stroked Seth's fur as she stared into his blue eyes. "You're beautiful," she whispered to him as he crouched down so she could mount him. She slowly climbed on his back before looking around.

"Justin, I swear if you drop me…" she heard Karina's voice say jokingly. She watched her aunt straighten herself on Justin's back. "I mean it, Gabi, your mother would be so proud of you." Gabriela smiled at her. Not wanting to say anything in fear of breaking down, she nodded at her. "So you ready?" she asked Gabriela. When Gabriela nodded, Karina chuckled. "Good because Seth says to hold on tight."

"Wait, you can hear him?" she asked.

Just as Karina opened her mouth to answer, Justin let out a howl before taking off into the woods with Seth close behind. She held on tightly as they zigzagged through the trees, howling at each other. Gabriela smiled and squealed as the wind blew through her hair. After running for about ten minutes, the pack made their way back to where the ceremony started. Seth crouched down so that Gabriela could climb off his back. She smiled at him as she hopped off, stroking his fur. "Thanks for the ride," she whispered before turning around so that he could shift back into his human self.

Seth cleared his throat loudly, letting Gabriela know it was safe to turn around. "So, Kitten…how was your first ride?" he asked as he pulled her into a hug.

"It was awesome." She pulled back as her aunt walked past with Justin. "Wait…how did you know what Seth said?" she asked her.

"Because I completed the process," she whispered, shooting her a wink, causing her to smile.

"Karina," growled Justin playfully. "You said you were going to wait to tell her." He smiled as they made their way back to the white runner.

"I was, but I was too excited to keep it in." She beamed with pride as she took her place in between Justin and Seth, with Gabriela on the other side of Seth. "She should know that there's nothing to be afraid of."

Seth smiled at his dad's new mate as the pack members made their way to them, bowing one by one to show their respect for their alphas and lunas. Once the last pack member showed their respects before returning back to the crowd, Seth and Gabriela turned to face Justin and Karina, bowing to show their respect to the current alpha and luna of the pack. It wasn't long after that when everyone made their way to the massive dining hall for their first official pack feast.

By the time it was over, Gabriela was exhausted. She stood up with a yawn and went to help some of the pack members who were clearing plates and folding up chairs. "Young Luna, you aren't required to clean up," said a woman to her with a bow, who looked to be in her forties.

Gabriela curtsied in return before taking the plate from the woman. "Just because it's not required doesn't mean I can't help." She smiled as she followed the woman from table to table, clearing away the dishes. Once all the tables were cleared, the woman bowed to Gabriela once again before excusing herself.

"You know you don't have to bow back, right?" said Seth with a smile as he pulled her into a hug.

"I know, but I want to. Why should they be the only ones to show respect? I want them to know I respect them just as much."

"You are something else, Kitten." He smiled as they headed toward the exit of the room.

"What about the rest of the cleaning up?"

"The rest will be done tomorrow. Besides, you've had a long day. You need to rest." He bowed playfully to her as she curtsied.

"Yes, my alpha," she said with a grin.

The two walked hand in hand toward the pack house in silence for a bit before Seth spoke. "You look gorgeous, Gabi."

She smiled. "If we get married, I want my dress to look just like this for my wedding. I never have worn anything so pretty in my life," she confessed.

Seth stopped and turned her to face him. "Gabi, what are you talking about? We just had our ceremony."

She looked at him confused. "I'm not saying you have to marry me," she joked. "I'm just saying that if we get married, I want—"

"Kitten, this *was* a wedding...*our* pack wedding." He looked at her with concern as he saw the panic in her face. "I thought you knew. Your aunt—"

"Seth, we are too young to get married! We haven't even finished high school yet!"

"Gabi, it's okay...it's not that big of a deal. Ceremonies like this happen all the time. Once you find your mate, if you have the training and knowledge, school is really a choice unless there's some type of special training or degree you want. Some people as young as—"

"No, Seth, it is a big deal! I'm not ready for this...you guys said I had time before we have to take over and—"

"Shhhhhh, calm down. Nothing has changed. Just because in this world we made that step...it doesn't mean anything else has to change." His tone was calm and soothing. He felt guilty that she didn't know what kind of ceremony this was. When Justin and Seth spoke to Karina about it, she said that she would take care of explaining the exact details to her.

"Seth, everything is different now. Once you're married, you have to have…" Her voice trailed off as she looked down at her fingers.

"Kitten, we don't do anything until you're ready," he assured her. He expected that after their magical ceremony, they'd be able to have a magical night, which would complete the mating process and the mate bond, but as much as it pained him to keep waiting, he wanted her to be ready to take that leap in her own time so that she was comfortable but most importantly happy. He kissed the crown of her head softly.

"Come on, it's late. Let's go," he said softly as he led her into the house.

Chapter 27

"Are you sure I should be here? I thought you said that this is for alphas only," said Gabriela as she and Seth followed Justin and Karina into the South Eclipse pack house for the yearly pack gatherings.

"No, I said that this was an alpha meeting... I never said it was for alphas only." He smiled as he guided her through to their great hall. "It's actually very important to have all major pack members present. That's how packs create and keep alliances."

Gabriela nodded in understanding as they patiently waited in line for their turn to bow to the hosting alpha and luna of the South Eclipse pack. She fidgeted nervously with her shirt with one hand as she looked around at the different members of other packs. When it was Seth and Gabriela's turn to bow in respect, she smiled nervously at the luna and alpha as she bowed with Seth.

"Welcome, young Seth," said Alpha Cole. "And congratulations on finding your mate." He smiled at them both. "I've heard of her heroics defending your pack before she was introduced. You should be proud of the choice the moon goddess has given you and your pack."

"Thank you, Alpha," responded Seth with a smile as he looked at his mate. "I'm grateful for her choice, more and more every day."

"Is it true that she is human?" he asked.

Gabriela flinched nervously as she waited for Seth to respond. "Yes, Alpha, she is. I wouldn't have her any other way."

"Congratulations, Young Luna, it's not every day that we hear of a human that has the nerve to take on a rogue wolf, let alone a whole pack."

"Thank you, Alpha," she said softly.

Alpha Cole smiled as he nodded in response as Seth led her away.

"Oh my god, Seth…that was so scary." She breathed out slowly as they followed the crowd and took their seats at their assigned tables.

"Come on, he wasn't scary," teased Seth as he kissed her cheek.

"You know what I mean… I'm not saying he was scary. I'm saying that this is scary." She motioned around at the room full of werewolves.

"Kitten, no one here would hurt you," he said softly to her.

"I'm not saying that they would… I just feel so out of place. What if I mess up and bow wrong or offend—"

"Calm down, you're doing fine. You heard Alpha Cole, and if he heard about what you did, everyone here has. You, Kitten, are respected here."

She smiled at her mate. Since the acceptance ceremony two months ago, she had spent most of her time learning about werewolves and their traditions. The only tradition she couldn't get past was the mating part. She knew that they would have to mate eventually, but she was scared. Having sex wasn't what scared her, it was the having sex with a werewolf part that scared her. She didn't know what to expect and was too embarrassed to ask. As she sat caught up in her thoughts, she didn't notice the involuntary growl that Seth let out. When he growled again, she was brought from her thoughts back to reality.

"Seth, what's wrong?" she asked.

"Gabi, your u—" he began before he was cut off.

"Your Uncle Diego is here, and he misses you," said a low, menacing voice behind her, causing her to shoot up from her seat and scramble behind Seth who took a defensive stance in front of her. "I have to say, Luna, you are everything I remember before your new pack killed your chosen mate," said Lucas's voice.

Gabriela clutched the back of Seth's shirt as she peeked around his large frame to see one of the men who helped string her up for her to be whipped when Max took her, standing in front of them along with Diego.

"He was never her mate," Seth spat through clenched teeth as he glared at the two men. "You would do well to remember that!"

"Gentlemen! This is a peace meeting!" boomed Alpha Cole's voice through the room. "There will not be any fighting here when we are to be making peace!" His gaze shifted from Seth to Lucas. "Take if off my land if you have a problem to settle." His tone was commanding.

"Yes, Alpha," responded Seth without breaking eye contact with Lucas.

"Thank you, Young Alpha, for your answer, but I wasn't speaking to you." Alpha Cole made his way from the head table on the raised platform to where Seth and Lucas stood. "I was speaking to you," he growled at Lucas, stepping in front of Seth.

"My apologies, Alpha." Lucas cockily bowed his head to Alpha Cole with a grin. "I meant no disrespect to you or your pack…it's just very upsetting to see another alpha with my dead alpha's mate."

Seth let out a feral growl for Alpha Cole to silence him. "Enough! You dare come into my territory and accuse other wolves of stealing mates? Who the hell do you think you are?" bellowed Alpha Cole.

"I'm Alpha Lucas…of the Red Rogues. My late alpha established our pack right before he was killed." He slowly raised his head. "An acquaintance of mine informed me that packs gather once a year to establish alliances to maintain claimed territory... and property."

"Your acquaintance informed you correctly, Alpha Lucas, but obviously, they didn't inform you of the rules, and I don't take kindly to disruptions. If you plan to be here as a pack alpha, learn the rules or get the hell off my land...do I make myself clear?"

"Yes, Alpha," responded Lucas. "Crystal."

"Good. You may register your pack with the secretary at the door. Once you're done, you will be escorted to a table...away from young Alpha Seth and *his* mate." Alpha Cole made sure to emphasize Seth's status and his mate. He had heard the rumors of the despicable treatment of Gabriela at the hands of Max, courtesy of a traitor in Justin's pack.

"Thank you, Alpha," said Lucas as he bowed again in submission. "My beta, Diego, would like a word with Gabriela and her aunt if she's here..." Lucas looked around to try and catch a glimpse of Justin and Karina. "They are his family after all."

"I will be sure to pass your request to Alpha Justin when he returns from his room. He will decide what he deems best. Now, please, register with my secretary." Alpha Cole watched as Lucas and who he now learned to be Diego made their way toward the back of the room to the pack secretary. Once he saw that she escorted them out of the room to do the tour of the pack lands, he turned to face Seth who held a sobbing Gabriela tightly to his chest.

"Are you okay?" he asked her.

She shook her head vigorously as she trembled with fear. "I-I-" she stuttered. "H-he w-was—"

"Kitten, look at me." Seth sat Gabriela in a chair and kneeled down so that he could look up at her face. "Gabi, I need for you to breathe, okay?"

She nodded as she tried to take slow breaths. Once her breathing slowed down enough for her to slow her shaking, she nodded again at Seth to let him know that she was doing better.

"Kitten, did you know that man?" She nodded slowly again at him. "Who is he?"

She shook her head. "No, I-I can't." She looked between Seth and Cole. "I'm sorry, sir... I—" She stood up to her feet and bowed to Cole, trying to recompose herself. "I didn't mean to cause a disruption in your pack."

"This wasn't your doing," said Cole to her. "There's no reason for you to apologize here." He motioned for his luna to join him. "Love, take her to my office to rest. Have the welcome meal changed to a general breakfast. We will change the official welcome to tonight," he said to his mate.

She nodded as she tried to guide Gabriela away from Seth. "Please don't make me leave him... please," she begged. "I can't lose him again... I won't survive."

"My dear, you're not leaving him," said the luna. "He's meeting us upstairs after he finds his father," she reassured Gabriela.

"Go, Gabi, I will be right behind you." Seth kissed her forehead before motioning for her to follow Cole's mate. When he saw her hesitate, he smiled. "Kitten, we are at the biggest werewolf convention in the United States. Alpha Cole has the most powerful pack around. You will be fine."

Gabriela nodded this time, giving Seth one final hug before following Cole's mate out of the hall. Cole cleared his throat, drawing Seth's attention from Gabriela to him. "It's obvious that she previously suffered a great deal at the hands of that pack…to the extent that I'm sure I can't even imagine," he said slowly. "With that being said, I cannot allow you to retaliate in revenge against them if they are here to negotiate peace."

"With all due respect, Alpha Cole, I will respect your wishes, and you're right…you can't imagine. I won't do anything against them as long as they stay away from us…from her. If he so much as breathes on her, I will kill him. I will kill them both."

Chapter 28

"Why didn't you link me right away?" asked Justin as they made their way to Alpha Cole's office.

"Dad, I knew you were busy and—"

"And what?" snapped Justin. "You should've let me know the moment you saw Diego!" He was furious that he had to explain to Karina how it was that Diego of all people had shown up at a peace treaty convention.

"Justin, please," Karina began.

"You two can growl at each other in your rooms with your mates later," said Cole.

He opened the door to his large office and walked over to the pack table where Gabriela and his mate were already waiting. He waited for everyone to find a seat before addressing the table. "We all are here because of a disruption downstairs between young Seth and Lucas from the Red Rogue Pack. I asked you all here to ask for insight about what led to what happened downstairs."

Justin sighed as he raked his hands through his hair. He looked at his mate before speaking.

"Alpha, I know this is your pack, but they shouldn't be here. I don't know who this Lucas person is that you and Seth are talking about, but Diego is my mate's ex-husband and Gabi's uncle. He was abusive to Karina and Gabi. He was dangerous enough as a human and is worse now that he's been turned."

Cole rubbed the stubble on his jaw. "This is the same Diego that attacked your pack with Max when he was killed?"

Justin nodded. He looked at Karina who was comforting Gabriela. "A member from my pack traded information with Max for information on Seth's mate. They used that information to use the human justice system as a funnel for information and power."

"Alpha Justin, I understand your frustration, but I cannot throw them out without cause or collaboration. I believe everything you're saying, but you know the rules. I need proof of a crime to present to the other packs. Even though this is my pack, with other packs present, we need to make sure that whatever decision is made, alliances can still be made."

Justin looked at his mate with pain in his eyes. He thought Diego would be smart enough to stay away from them but obviously not. "I can't ask them to relive what they went through." He sighed. "It wouldn't be fair of me to ask them to."

Karina reached for Justin's hands. "Yes, you can," she said softly. "I let Diego ruin my relationship with the only family I had left. His control over me let my niece think the worst of me, and that stops today." She ran her hand through Gabriela's hair, causing her to look at her aunt. "I'm so sorry I let him control me like that. I put you in more danger every day that he used you against me." She turned toward Cole. "If you need proof of a crime, then I will be your proof."

"No," whispered Gabriela softly. "We will be your proof or..." Gabriela paused as she looked at her aunt before smiling. "I can be your proof." She pulled her sweater over her head, leaving her in her cami, and turned around, showing her back to Cole and his mate, causing her to gasp.

"Oh my goddess, child...what did they do to you?" she asked in shock as she clutched Cole's hands.

"They whipped me...well Max did," she said softly. She sighed sadly as Seth growled. "The man, Lucas, actually helped tie me up to the posts..." After she was sure that the alpha and luna had seen enough of her back, she turned and flipped her wrists out so that they could see the brands on the inside of her wrists. "He also gave Max the poker to brand me...he held me in place...he held me still," she choked out, "so that he could mark me as his property." She pulled her sweater back over her head. "As for my uncle, well he left plenty of scars if you need to see those too even though most of them have healed." She smiled sadly as she raised her head to look around the table.

"Alpha and Luna, the physical scars aren't the problem..." said Karina, standing next to her niece. "It's the ones you can't see that are the most heinous."

"I'm afraid I don't follow," said Cole's mate. "What can be worse than what the young luna has shown us?" She shuddered as she imagined poor Gabriela being burned, beaten, and whipped.

"Alpha, you said that you heard about what happened when Justin's pack was attacked, right?" asked Gabriela.

"Yes, it spread like wildfire from pack to pack," he responded. "Why?"

"Did you hear about what happened before? About how Seth found me?" She waited for Cole to answer, but he shook his head. "They got to me just in time and saved me from Diego. This last time that he beat me was different because he tried to rape me." She took a slow breath to keep calm as she continued talking. "He beat me so bad that I didn't even know if he did or not..."

"You poor child," said Cole's mate as she clutched her chest with one hand and grabbed Cole with the other. "How could someone so young suffer so much?" She looked at Cole with a stern look on her face. "They are to leave...they don't belong here."

"Love, I know that she's suffered at the hands of these men, but they will want the right to defend themselves..."

"Cole, nothing they say can defend what they've done." She crossed her arms across her chest. "Fine, *if* and only if the young luna agrees to it, they can stay and explain themselves. They must publicly confess to the packs here every misdeed that they've committed if they plan to stay. *If* they agree, they will abide by our rules as long as they are here."

Cole ran his hands down his face at his mate's ultimatum. "Love, please...if we do that, we will be singling them out. They will think we aren't honest about trying to discuss alliances here if it appears we are playing favorites."

"Colton, I swear to the moon goddess that if you do anything different from what I just said, you will regret it!" growled Cole's mate. "I will not have you catering to them as if they are some misunderstood misfits! And if they are innocent, they should have no problem with what I am suggesting."

"Please, Luna, I don't want to cause problems in your pack. Please, don't fight with your mate because of me." Gabriela couldn't help but feel guilty that she was the cause of their argument.

"Dear child, you have so much to learn." Cole's mate smiled at Gabriela. "Situations like this are why we hold these conventions every year...never have we heard of a situation as extreme as yours, but when packs like this go unchallenged, they never stop once they start. Packs, especially new alphas and lunas need to know who they can rely on for support. My dear mate seems to have forgotten... that's all."

"Fine, love...you win. We will hold the meeting after the welcome dinner tonight." He grinned at his mate. "You are a force to be reckoned with."

"I know." She smiled as she gave Cole a kiss.

Once the particulars of the meeting were discussed, Seth, Gabriela, Justin, and Karina excused themselves from the office and headed back down to the dining hall in silence. No one knew what to say to each other after leaving the office. When the silence became unbearable, Justin let out a small growl of annoyance.

"Look, I didn't mean to blow up the way I did, but you need to understand that you can't keep things like that to yourself. I know you're my son and you worry about your mate just like I do, but you are the future alpha of our pack...you need to think like one."

Seth nodded as he and Gabriela trailed behind his dad. He knew his dad was right about his behavior, but he also wanted to prove to Gabriela that he could defend and protect his mate and make her feel safe. As the dining hall doors opened for them to enter, a scent triggered Seth to let out a growl.

"Seth? What's wrong? What is it?" asked Gabriela.

"Jessica."

Chapter 29

"Alphas and lunas, thank you for agreeing to this gathering. I have called this gathering because of a disagreement that most of you witnessed today between two packs at the morning feast," announced Cole. "Since we all have gathered here in the name of peace, only when the air is clear can peace be made. With that being said, every pack here is expected to behave certain standards, and if you don't have them, then you need to get them."

He turned toward Lucas and Diego. "As new-comers, do you, Alpha Lucas, meet the standards?"

Lucas smiled as he stood up. "Alpha, I'm sure you have already heard exaggerated stories…and no, I and my pack don't meet your standards yet, but I plan to meet them soon."

"I'm sure you do, Alpha," responded Cole as he motioned for his mate to speak.

"Don't worry, Alpha Lucas, you will have every opportunity to meet those standards right now. When a pack comes to a peace gathering, they must come with nothing to cause conflicts…that way peace can be promoted. Now, here before these packs, you have the opportunity to discuss what could hold your pack back from meeting the standards."

Lucas's smile quickly changed from a smile to a frown. "I'm sorry, but I don't think I understand what you're suggesting, Luna."

"I'm suggesting if there is anything that would keep your pack from being able to enter into an alliance with any pack that is represented in this room, speak now so it won't be used against you in the future."

"Ahhhh, I understand. You mean because of my late alpha and his chosen luna over there." Lucas smugly grinned as he looked in Gabriela's direction. "Yes, well…let me explain. The alpha who founded my pack was offered a human girl to be the luna of our pack by a pack member from Alpha Justin's pack and Diego here when he was human. There seems to be some confusion about who her mate is since Alpha Max is dead, but there never is any confusion about a mate when he or she is marked, and she, ladies and gentlemen, was marked by my alpha before he was killed, which makes her the chosen luna of our pack." Lucas looked around the room before continuing, "After killing my alpha, our chosen luna was taken and made the future luna to his pack."

Cole narrowed his eyes at Lucas, unbelieving how careful he was with his words when answering to the packs. "So you're saying that young Gabriela chose your alpha willingly?"

"I'm saying that the choice was made for her by her legal guardian appointed by the human court of law. She was a minor, so it wasn't her choice to make. The choice Diego made for her was in the best interest of her safety and well-being," said Lucas.

"Are you serious?" shouted Gabriela as she shot up from her seat. "My best interest?"

"Gabi," said Seth to her. He expected for Lucas to lie and try to antagonize him into an altercation, but he never imagined Gabriela responding the way she was right now. He pulled on her arm as he tried to get her attention. He wasn't sure if this was a diversion for something. He warned his father and Alpha Cole that he had smelled Jessica's scent earlier and that their coming here could easily be a trap. "Kitten, come on. Sit—"

"No!" she screamed. "How dare you!" she shouted in Lucas's and Diego's direction. "How dare you," she said again louder. "My best interest?" She pulled her sweater from over her head, exposing her scars to the room. "You call this choice in the best interest of my safety and well-being? Being strung up and whipped was for my safety?" she spat as she ignored all the gasps from around her. "What about being whipped or branded is safe?" she asked as she thrusted her hands out so that the palms or her hands were facing up, exposing the brand that Max inflicted on her. "You make it sound like you—"

"I understand that what the late alpha did was extreme, but the person who did those things was killed by your new mate's father. I wasn't the one who did those things to you," Lucas said.

Gabriela snorted. "You're right, *you* weren't the one who did those things. *You* were the one who helped him. *You* were the one who hung me up for him! *You* were the one who held me still so he could brand me like cattle!" she screamed, causing everyone in the room to shoot glares at Lucas. "And you!" she pointed at Diego, ignoring the obvious rage on their faces. "Wasn't it bad enough that you beat me…then try to rape me but giving me away so that you could be like him?"

Seth pulled Gabriela into a hug as he tried to calm her down. After a few moments, she let out a slow breath. She pulled her sweater back on and ran her hands through her hair to compose herself before turning to Cole and his mate.

"Alpha, Luna… I apologize for my outburst," she said as she bowed. She raised her head and looked around at all the shocked faces around her. "I apologize to you all for my behavior," she bowed again briefly and took her seat next to Seth.

Cole and his mate nodded at Gabriela, accepting her apology, but it was the luna who spoke. "Child, you have no reason to apologize. It takes bravery to do what you just did here. You suffered a great deal. Much more than any werewolf in this room." She smiled softly at Gabriela. "With that being said," she turned her gaze to Lucas and Diego, "this is a gathering for alliances to be made, and I have to say, gentlemen, that what I just heard makes me wonder if you will be able to form alliances with any pack here with what was just said."

Lucas looked around at the hard faces around him. "I understand, but I was only following the orders of my alpha. As you all know here, an alpha's order is law," he protested as he tried to think of a new plan. He wasn't expecting for Gabriela to grow a backbone strong enough to expose that about them or herself.

"Yes, an alpha's order is law," began Cole. "But that is why we have our pack...our second- and third-in-command. It is the responsibility of those close to the alpha to guide and support the alpha. Are you saying you don't agree with what he did to her?" asked Cole. Not giving him a change to respond, he continued, "Because if you didn't agree, you could've left or challenged him. You did neither."

"I see everyone has already made up their minds about me," he said. "I find it unfair that I'm on trial for what Max did. Don't I get the opportunity to prove myself that I can run my pack differently?" He could see some of the other alphas in the room nod. "All packs start somewhere, and I know not all packs start with happy beginnings. I'm asking for a chance to correct the wrongs that obviously caused so much pain."

Gabriela rolled her eyes at Lucas. She looked around at some of the people nodding at Lucas as others shook their heads. She leaned into Seth and whispered, "They can't be seriously buying this, can they?" she asked.

"I don't know," he responded as he looked across the table at his father. All it took was enough people to believe he was sincere for him to earn a place at the peace pact to give him access to the same defense options and alliances that his father had set up.

"Then it's settled," said Cole as he looked around. "You all have heard both the accuser and the accused speak. You saw the marks on her body that he admits were administered by the previous alpha of his pack. The scars we saw are not to be taken lightly." Heads around the room nodded as he continued to speak, "I believe a vote is in order to decide Alpha Lucas's eligibility to remain here." He cleared his throat. "If you believe Alpha Lucas deserves the right at a chance of peace and a new start, stand." He watched some individuals raise to their feet as his mate counted the ones standing. "If you feel his involvement taking orders should be held against him, stand." His heart sank as he saw the look on his mate's face. It was a look of disgust. He knew what that look was for. He looked over at Lucas who had an evil grin on his face. The majority were in favor of Lucas staying.

Chapter 30

Gabriela sat on the edge of the bed in the room she shared with Seth, fuming in anger. She felt an unfamiliar feeling of courage and anger that appeared after her outburst at Lucas. "How could they not see he was lying?" she said to Seth who only shook his head.

"Because they have to consider who to make alliances with," responded Justin, who held Karina tightly. "Some packs have different outlooks and beliefs than us."

She shook her head in annoyance. "I don't understand how they are letting him act like he's innocent...he admitted to it."

Seth pulled Gabriela into a hug. He liked seeing this feisty side of his mate but hated that she was upset. "Because in a pack, everyone has to obey the alpha. It's like a rule...a law." He looked to his father for help to better explain so that she would understand.

"Gabi, packs have hierarchies. The alpha is kind of like a king, so to speak. When an alpha gives an order, it has to be followed. It's almost impossible to ignore the order, but that doesn't mean that there aren't ways around one."

"What do you mean?"

"For example, if a member receives an order from an alpha, they must follow the order or leave the pack," Justin replied. "Loyalty and obedience are vital to a pack's success and survival."

"So since they gave him a clean slate, do I need to be near them like nothing happened? Because I have no intentions—"

"No, Alpha Cole made it clear that since he is allowed to stay, he and Diego are to avoid you and your aunt."

She spun her ring around her finger as she lost herself in her thoughts, oblivious to Justin and Karina leaving the room.

"Kitten," came Seth's voice softly from behind her, snapping her from her thoughts. "Kitten," he said again as he pulled her into a hug. "You're warm," he said as he hugged her.

"I know," she responded softly as she nuzzled into his chest. She could feel herself going into heat at the meeting when her outburst happened.

"You're going into heat," he breathed huskily as he inhaled her scent.

"I know." She pulled her sweater over her head slowly as he stroked her cheek. "Seth," she breathed nervously. "When we go home…when we go home,

I—" She took a nervous breath to gather the nerves to finish her sentence. "I want to finish the process. I'm ready."

Seth froze at her words. "W-what? Are you sure? Because we can wait. I don't want you to feel obligated. Don't feel like you have to if you still aren't comfortable."

"I-I'm sure," she responded as she pulled him in for a kiss. "This will be the last time I go into heat."

Seth could feel his wolf's excitement as he passionately kissed her. He waited for so long to hear her say she was ready to take the next step.

"Kitten, I love you so much." His eyes began to change as he whispered to her, trailing his kisses down to her neck.

"I love you too," she moaned as he sucked on her mark. "I love you so much, Seth!" she screamed out when his teeth pierced her skin. They hugged each other tightly as the wave of emotions passed through them both.

Once they came down off their wave of pleasure, they laid down on the bed, tangled in each other's embrace. "Kitten, if you change your mind when we get home, I'll understand."

"No, Seth. I'm not going to change my mind. I know I will probably be horrible at it because I don't know what I'm—"

Seth pulled out of the embrace enough so that they could see each other's faces. "Don't you dare finish that sentence. You will be fine," he assured her. "And I like that you won't know what you're doing. That means I will be your first…and you will be my last."

Chapter 31

Gabriela and Seth sat at their assigned tables while Alpha Cole gave his final presentation to all the attending packs before dismissing them to mingle with other packs to form alliances. Seth's grip around Gabriela tightened when she tried to reach for her drink.

"Seth, you're going to crush me." She giggled.

"I can't help it. You smell so good." He kept his eyes on Alpha Cole as he inhaled her scent. "Besides, your heat hasn't died down yet. You still have a while before it does, and I can't have other males thinking you're available," he whispered.

She swatted at him playfully. "Seth, I'm marked. Anyone can see that, now let go." She leaned forward as his grip loosened. "Besides, last night was the last time you will ever have to mark me."

Seth smiled at Gabriela as she leaned back into him. They listened to the ending to Alpha Cole's speech before standing. He could tell that Gabriela was uneasy being in the same room with Max's predecessor and wanted her to feel as safe as possible.

He placed a soft kiss to the top of her head when he heard a voice from behind him. It was a voice he despised.

"Hey, guys! Long time no see!" said Jessica as she flashed a smile. "I wanted to apologize for my behavior." She stood on the tip of her toes as she looked around. "Have you seen Alpha Justin? I want to give him my apologies also."

Gabriela grabbed Seth's arm as he growled out. "You have some nerve coming up to us!"

"Alpha," she bowed. "I admit I was wrong. I was jealous, but I see you made your choice...even *if* you two aren't mated yet."

The spitefulness in her tone didn't go unnoticed. "It's none of your business whether *my* mate and I mated or not." He narrowed his eyes at her as she smiled. "What are you doing here?"

"My new pack is here. I was brought along as their secretary." Her tone was regretful for a moment but quickly changed. "My alpha asked me to meet every pack here before he meets with them."

"Good, now leave," he spat. He turned away from Jessica but stopped. "Who is the pack you're here with?"

"Alpha Lucas. Apparently, Alpha Cole has my alpha under restrictions while he's here so that's why I'm meeting everyone first."

"You mean trying to intimidate me?" said Gabriela as she tugged on Seth's arm.

Jessica's eyes flashed a bright shade of red momentarily before returning to their normal color. "Alpha Cole said Diego and Lucas couldn't come near you. He said nothing about me." Her eyes flashed again. "Besides. I'm only talking to you because I'm supposed to be looking for potential allies, and you...you're not strong enough to protect a puppy," she spat at Gabriela before looking at Seth. "I will tell Lucas you obviously aren't interested in a deal. Maybe, your dad will want one." She flipped her hair as she spun around and strutted away.

"I hate her," growled Seth.

"Seth, she's not worth it. Come on. Let's go." She pulled on Seth's arm. "You said we have to meet new people."

He nodded as he allowed her to lead him away. "You are going to make a great luna," he said to her.

Seth and Gabriela made their way around the room, introducing themselves to other alphas and lunas. After a few hours, they made their way to Justin and Karina, who was laughing with a nearby couple.

"Seth, Gabi! Meet Trevor and his mate, Mara. They were good friends with your mother," he said to Seth. "You and their son used to play together all the time when you were pups."

Seth bowed briefly. "How are you?" he asked. He remembered hearing wonderful stories about Trevor and Mara but never their son.

"Good, congratulations on finding your mate. She's gorgeous," said Mara, causing Gabriela to blush. "You all really should come visit us! I'm sure Damien would love to see you and catch up, Seth."

"Yeah, maybe you could help him get back on track...for the pack," said Trevor sadly. "He's been rebellious lately."

"Yeah, maybe..." Seth glanced at his dad.

Damien had become the rebel of their pack, opening them up for attacks and betrayals. The few times that they've come across each other, it was at pack parties or clubs, and he wasn't the friendliest.

"Great! It's settled! After the convention, you can come with us and stay as our guests!" squealed Mara.

Seth nervously looked at Justin. "The kids can go, but unfortunately, I left the pack in the hands of my beta and his son. I've been gone for too long," said Justin.

Dad, I don't want to go. You know his reputation! linked Seth to Justin. *Gabi's in heat, and he's not mated! I can't take Gabi around him!*

Seth, you are an alpha! It's time you start acting like one. he responded. *You're going because the current luna and alpha invited you.*

Seth squeezed Gabriela's hand as he closed the link with his dad. This was not what he and Gabriela had planned at all. They were planning to go home and finish the mating process, not to be hanging out with a spoiled pack brat. After saying their good-byes, Seth and Gabriela headed to their room to pack their belongings.

"Seth, what's wrong? You've been acting weird since we met Trevor and Mara…"

"It's nothing, Kitten. I just really don't care much for their son. He's not someone I want to bring you around. You're in heat, and he doesn't have a mate."

"Seth, relax. Plus, I'm marked by my true mate. And you heard them. Maybe, you can help get him on track." She zipped her suitcase and pulled it off the bed onto the ground. "Maybe, this is a good thing."

"You are too trusting." He kissed her cheek before grabbing her bag and pulling it toward the door. "Besides, with Lucas and Jessica teamed up, you shouldn't be anywhere without guards or—"

"Seth, I'm with you. I'm not worried and, obviously, neither is your dad." She slid past Seth out the front door.

"And to think you were worried you wouldn't know how to act around wolves," he muttered as he closed the door behind him. He smiled at his mate. She had become comfortable with wolves and herself enough to find herself. He followed her down the stairs to the crowded lobby where everyone was hugging and saying their farewells. After a few hugs and handshakes, they made their way outside to their car where Trevor and Mara already were waiting.

"You have no idea how excited we are to have you both. It's been too long!" Mara pulled her phone out. "I'm texting Damien now. He will be so happy to see you."

"Mara, if you keep talking, we will be here forever," said Trevor. "Seth, do you need to speak to your dad before you go?"

He shook his head. "Dad and Karina came by early this morning. They had a long drive, so they left before we came down."

"Great. Let's hit the road then." He flashed a grin as he got into his car with Mara.

He and Mara knew that Seth didn't want to go, but Seth didn't know that this was Justin's idea. He and Karina were already unsure of Lucas's intentions, but with Jessica showing up, he was even more uneasy. As he started the car up and put into gear, he pulled out and checked his rearview mirror.

"I feel horrible for misleading them this way," said Mara. "They have a right to know."

"Please, don't start this again." Trevor sighed as he gripped the steering wheel. "Justin doesn't want to worry them."

"Worrying them and lying to them are two different things." She huffed as she crossed her arms. "They won't be prepared if something were to happen because—"

"Mara, please! This isn't our choice to make whether we agree to it or not. Please, don't make this any harder than it needs to be."

"Fine, I will keep quiet, but the first sign of trouble... I'm telling them. They deserve to know that Lucas plans on attacking them with that traitorous pack sl—"

"Mara! What's gotten into you? Since when do you talk like that?"

"Since that girl had the courage to stand up for herself in that room and confront them about what they did to her! That girl has the body of a human but the heart of a wolf, and for her to be treated like that..." She closed her eyes and took a breath. "Trevor, Damien used to hang with that girl. He brought her into our pack...into our home! How do we know Jessica won't do the same to us? Look what she did to her own pack!"

"I was thinking the same thing. That's why when we get back, we are going to have a meeting. All of us. I've been too lenient with him and letting him do as he pleases. After tonight, he has no choice. He's going to start behaving like an alpha."

Chapter 32

"Woah, Seth, long time no see," said Damien as Seth and Gabriela followed Trevor and Mara into their pack house. "The last time I saw you, you were hookin' up with that blond piece of a—"

"Hey! Damien, meet my mate, Gabriela," interrupted Seth nervously. He tensed as Gabriela reached to shake Damien's hand when his eyes traveled to her neck.

"Nice to meet you. You know, you're famous in the wereworld," he grinned at her as Seth threw an arm around her shoulder. "Dad says you guys are hanging out here for a while." His eyes never left hers as he spoke.

"Yeah, your parents suggested we catch up." Seth laughed, breaking Damien's trance.

"We haven't been out to the club together in forever…wanna go into town?" asked Damien after he sniffed the air before pulling out his cell phone.

"I don't know, man. We've been driving for a while, Gabi?" he asked as he noticed Damien sniffing the air again. He could feel his wolf becoming agitated at Damien's demeanor. Him sniffing the air meant he could smell that Gabriela was in heat, which was exactly what he didn't want happening.

"Sure!" she squealed. "I've never been to a club before."

"Awesome. Seth used to go there a lot. I'm surprised he never took you." Damien winked at Gabriela before heading into the kitchen where his mom and dad were.

"Kitten, when we get there…stay with me at all times, okay? And don't take drinks from anyone you don't know."

"Seth, I know I'm sheltered, but we learned all about stranger danger a long time ago." She giggled as he pulled her into his chest.

"Kitten, clubs aren't what you're used to." He smiled at her as Damien exited the kitchen with Trevor and Mara.

"So, you kids are going out?" asked Trevor with a grin.

"Yeah, apparently, Seth's mate has never been out to a club."

"Which is a good thing." Mara swatted at Damien playfully. "You'll be careful," she said to Damien in more of a demanding tone than a question. When he nodded as he grabbed his keys, she shouted behind him. "Behave yourself!" She turned to Seth and Gabriela who were still standing in the room. "You two, have fun…not too much fun though."

"Yes, Luna," said Gabriela nervously.

"Gabi, we are Mara and Trevor to you both… no need for formalities," said Mara to her with a smile.

"Yes ma'am. I mean—"

"It's okay," said Trevor. "I'm sure this takes some getting used to. Go on before Damien thinks you guys ditched him for us."

Gabriela and Seth headed out the door after their goodbyes and climbed into Seth's car. They followed Damien's car down the driveway before turning onto the main road to make the hour drive to the nightclub. He parked the car and quickly exited the car as Gabriela slid out of the passenger side with a huge smile on her face as she stared at the bright neon lights before her.

"Wow! You used to come here?" she asked Seth as he placed his hand on the small of her back as they followed Damien into the club.

They made their way to the front of the line and were waved through and headed up the stairs to the second floor VIP section.

"What are you guys drinking?" yelled Damien over the loud music.

"Coke please," yelled Gabriela as she looked around the club. She moved out from under Seth's arm and walked over to the railing. She nodded her head to the beat of the music as she watched the bodies down below swaying and moving against each other. When she saw the waitress come back with the drinks, she headed back over to Seth. "Can we go dance?" she asked.

"Sure," he yelled as he stood up. "Take your drink with you."

He waited for her to grab her cup before leading her down the stairs onto the floor. He found a spot on the floor but close enough to the steps before turning to face his mate with a smile. He wrapped his arms around her waist as she threw one arm around his neck and swayed to the music, setting her cup down on the counter near the stairs. They lost themselves in each other and the music with each song that came over the speakers. After a long period of dancing and a few make-out sessions, they made their way back to the VIP section where Damien sat with an unreadable look on his face.

"You sure you never came to a club before?" Damien asked Gabriela as they took their seats. He smiled as she shook her head no. "Well, I couldn't tell." He grinned at Seth who was glaring at him. "I ordered us drinks. The waitress will be back with them soon."

Seth only nodded as he kept a secure arm around Gabriela as she continued to nod to the beat, oblivious to the tension between him and Damien. He was anxious for Gabriela's heat to be over so that he

didn't feel so on edge around other unmated males…
especially unmated alphas. He leaned into her as she
relaxed into his side.

"Are you having fun?" he asked her.

She nodded. "It's nice…but I don't know if I
could do this all the time though. It's too loud," she
confessed with a smile.

"I'm glad," he said to himself as he pulled his
ringing cell phone from his pocket. "Kitten, I gotta
take this. It's Jace." He held his hand out for her to
follow him, but she shook her head.

"I'll wait for you here. I promise I won't go anywhere." She pouted at the unsure look on Seth's face.
"Damien's here, he will look after me until you get
back."

He growled out a little. "I won't be long," he
assured her. "Remember, no drinks from—"

"Yes, I know. No drinks from strangers and stay
put." She placed a soft kiss to his lips before he stood
up.

"I won't be long." He glanced quickly at Damien
before heading down the stairs

Damien watched Seth make his way through
the crowd before speaking to Gabriela. "So, you're
his mate… I never thought I'd see big bad Seth settle," he joked as the waitress returned with a tray of
drinks.

She nodded. "He's the best thing that ever happened to me. Literally."

"So I've heard. When are you guys going to mate?" he asked casually as he handed her a glass before taking a sip of his drink.

She felt herself blush at his question. "Um… uh-how did you…how do you know?" she stammered.

"Seth's behavior…and your scent. You're in heat."

She took a gulp of the sweet beverage as she scrambled for something to say. "Well, we are going to as soon as we get home." She took another gulp as she felt herself slowly relaxing. "This juice is really good," she said, changing the subject.

"Yeah, it is." He grinned at her as he tried to analyze her personality. "Are there a lot of available females in his pack?"

Gabriela shrugged her shoulders as she drained the glass of its contents. "I only know of a few, why?"

"My dad wants me to get serious about taking over… I need to find my mate." He handed Gabriela another glass as she nodded in understanding. "I actually thought his little traitor was my mate, but I had to wait until her birthday to find out. Now she's gone."

Gabriela felt a wave of sadness as she let his words sink in. Jessica was so desperate for her mate that she was willing to betray her whole pack and here was someone who thought she was his mate. "Damien, I'm so sorry. Maybe, you can tell her and save her. The new pack she's with is horrible, and she seems like she wasn't always a bad person," she slurred.

"You sound like you care about her." Damien leaned back into the leather couch as he considered Gabriela's words. "She's done horrible things. I don't know if I could accept someone like that as my mate."

Gabriela giggled. "I didn't know if I could accept Seth after everything, but I did. You know why?" she asked, unaware of Seth's presence coming up the steps with Jace close behind. "Because I love Seth. I got to know him and he is the bestess person I have ever meeted."

"Thank you, Kitten," he said as he cautiously sat down next to her. He glared at Damien, letting his eyes glow before returning them back to their normal color. "You got her drunk?" he growled.

"She's not drunk, relax. She might be tipsy but—"

"But what? As soon as I turn my back, you get my mate drunk to take advantage of her? What the hell Dame?" he yelled as she stood up from next to Gabriela and started walking toward Damien.

"Seth, stop! He wasn't doing anything! We were just talking!" She looked at Jace for help who just stood there with an annoyed look on his face. "Jace! Do something!" she screamed as she jumped in front of Seth.

"Calm down, man," Jace said as he stood behind Gabriela, blocking Seth's view of Damien. "She was telling him how much she loves you when we got here. Maybe, they were just talking," reasoned Jace.

Gabriela staggered back a few steps as she looked at Seth. "You don't trust me?" she asked.

"Baby, you know I do. It's *him* I don't trust," he admitted. "Kitten, I should—"

"Should trust me enough to ask me if you have any doubts instead of picking a fight!" she yelled. "If you wanted to know, you could've just asked."

"Kitten, please." He reached for her arm as she yanked herself free before stumbling a little before catching her balance.

"You want to know what we were talking about?" she yelled. "Mates! About how much I love you and how you saved me and how he thinks Jessica could be his mate!" Both Seth and Jace's heads whipped in Damien's direction with shocked expressions on their face. "You are the best thing that happened to me, Seth, and it's not fair of you to assume the worst about someone who only wants the same thing as you!"

Seth's expression softened at his mate's words. He never considered anything from anyone else's point of view. "Kitten, I'm sorry. I didn't mean to upset you." He reached for her but stopped as she pulled away from him once again.

"Don't apologize to me. You apologize to your friend first! I'm not the one you accused of something wrong." She turned toward Jace who was shocked at Gabriela's liquid lecture that she gave Seth.

"Jace, take be mack to Trevor and Mara... I mean make me tack..." She stomped her foot as she struggled to get the words out. "Ugh! You know what I mean!" She swayed past Seth who could only grin at his mate.

"Spoken like a true luna," he said to himself as he watched his soon-to-be beta lead his mate down the stairs. He let out a sigh because, unfortunately, he knew Gabriela was right. Clearing his throat, he walked over to Damien.

"Damien, man... I owe you an apology."

Chapter 33

Gabriela rolled over with a groan and a pounding headache. She opened her eyes and quickly shut them again. "Oh my god, I feel horrible," she whined as she sat herself up from the bed.

She looked around the room and saw a few pills and a glass of water on the nightstand next to the bed. Without a second thought, she grabbed the pills and downed them before slowly standing to her feet. She shuffled to the bathroom and hurriedly took a shower as she went over the events from last night. After brushing her teeth and getting dressed, she slowly made her way downstairs to the kitchen where Seth and Damien sat with Trevor and Mara.

"Good morning, did you have a good time?" Mara sipped on her coffee, waiting for Gabriela to answer.

"I did…" she answered as she took her seat near Seth, who slid his coffee in front of her. "I just didn't know I'd wake up feeling this bad," she groaned, causing Trevor and Mara to laugh.

"Anytime you drink too much alcohol, you wake up with a hangover." Trevor laughed.

"Alcohol?" she asked, confused. "I don't drink… I can't… I'm not old enough."

"Yeah, about that…" Damien rubbed the back of his neck. "I thought you knew the drinks I gave you were mixed…"

"Wait, what? The juice was mixed? With what?" She searched her thoughts but only remembered the soda and juice. "The juice tasted like juice." She frowned as she tried to put together what he was saying. She had heard stories about the nasty tastes of alcohol and her drink last night was anything but.

"It was mixed with alcohol. I thought—"

"You thought what?" she yelled. "I took up for you last night."

"I know, and I'm sorry. I didn't know you never drank before. I was just trying to find common ground for us to talk."

"We had it before you handed me that cup!" she shouted.

"It was wrong. Believe me, Seth made that very clear after he apologized last night."

"Apologized?" She turned to Seth who looked like a little boy in time-out.

"Yeah, I don't know how much of last night you remember, but you were right… Gabi, I was wrong to assume the worst the way I did." He motioned around the table. "That's why we were discussing pack alliances and strategies because a very smart luna told me last night that it wasn't fair of me to assume stuff."

She felt herself flush. "Yeah, I didn't mean to yell at you last night."

"You were right, Kitten. Everyone deserves the chance to be happy. Is it true you told him to find her?" he asked. He couldn't bring himself to say Jessica's name.

She nodded. "If she is his mate…or anyone's mate, that might be what she needs to see—that what she's doing is wrong. I know she's done horrible things, but I've seen her face when she thought no one was looking."

"What do you mean?" asked Damien. He looked around the table at the sad faces before him. Aside from stories of her heroics, he's heard of vague stories about her being abused before Seth's pack took her in but never anything saying how or by who.

"I mean when she watched me get whipped, her face said what her voice couldn't. She looked disgusted…and scared."

"Excuse me? Whipped?" Damien spat. "She watched them do it?" He shook his head. "I'm sorry, but if she did that, then there's no way she's my mate. I don't care if the goddess made her for me."

"Damien, I know it sounds bad, but—"

"Are you serious, Gabriela? How can you defend her?" He shot up out of his seat. "I can't have a known traitor as my mate. I won't."

"Damien, please. I'm not saying you have to. I'm just saying to see her to see if you are mates. If you are her mate, she could come back from whatever made her go to them in the first place."

Damien looked at Seth. "Dude, are you listening to your mate right now?"

Seth shrugged his shoulders. "Yeah, and believe me. As much as I hate her defending her, she might be right. Jace told me last night that he heard his dad talking to my dad about Lucas attacking the pack. Dad only sent us here to keep us away in case …"

Mara shot a glare at Trevor. "I warned you they would find out," she snapped.

Damien, Seth, and Gabriela all looked at Trevor and Mara. "Mom, what are you talking about?"

"Alpha Justin was warned by another alpha that he heard Lucas and Diego talking about attacking shortly after the convention was over." Trevor ran his hand through his hair before continuing. "Your dad knew you wouldn't have left if you knew."

"He's right, I wouldn't have." Seth stood up and pulled his phone out to dial Jace. "I have to go. If they're attacking, my dad will need us."

Trevor sighed. "Seth, your dad doesn't want you anywhere near the pack. Even though Max is dead, no one knows Lucas's plan."

"I can't abandon them. They're my pack too!"

"Seth, please calm down." Gabriela reached for his hand, but he was already heading toward the door. "Seth, wait!" She chased him through the room and outside to where Jace was standing. "Seth, just call Justin before you make a decision."

Seth gave his mate a soft look as Damien arrived outside with his parents.

"Look, Seth, how about I go with you to your pack and help you check out stuff there." He looked at his parents who nodded nervously. "Gabriela can stay here...just to be safe."

"No, that's a negative. I'm not staying here. I have to check on the kids at the orphanage," she pouted.

"Kitten, Damien's right. You're safer here until they're taken care of. I'm not risking your safety." He ran his finger down her cheek as she shed a tear. "I promise I will come back for you."

Gabriela took a step back and wiped her tear-stained face. "You better." She watched Jace, Seth, and Damien climb into the SUV and speed away. "Please, come back to me," she whispered as the tail light disappeared into the distance.

Chapter 34

"Honey, please sit down. You need to relax," suggested Mara as Gabriela paced back and forth in the pack kitchen. "I know you're worried, but it doesn't do any good to pace a hole in the floor."

Gabriela sighed. "It's been hours. Why haven't they responded to us?" She checked her phone again. "I know you said these things take time, but something's wrong. Something doesn't feel right." She ran her hand through her hair.

"How about you head upstairs and try to rest. If we hear something, we'll come get you." Trevor tried to offer a supportive smile to help encourage her to take him up on his suggestion.

After a few moments, she reluctantly nodded before turning toward the doorway. "Thank you, both of you, for looking after me until he gets back," she said softly. She walked out of the room and headed up the stairs, but a howl near the house caused her to stop in her tracks. She waited a few moments when she heard another howl followed by a growl before running down the stairs. "Mara! Trevor!"

"Gabriela! Run!" came Mara's strained voice.

That was all she needed to hear. She pulled her cell phone out of her pocket and ran toward the front door. "Come on, Seth, pick up," she pleaded as she bolted for a nearby garage. When he didn't answer, she sent him a text. She let herself in the garage and slid into the driver side of a Chevy Suburban. "God, I'm stealing a car...please forgive me for doing this." She put the keys in the ignition and turned on the SUV.

As the garage doors opened, she flicked on the lights but let out a cry at what the headlights illuminated. There stood Lucas, Diego, and Jessica holding Trevor and Mara with blades to their necks.

"Turn off the car and get out!" ordered Lucas. He tightened his grip on Mara, yanking her head back. "Don't make me repeat myself, little girl," he growled.

Gabriela turned the car off and slowly opened the door.

"You get back in that car right now!" yelled Mara.

Gabriela shook her head. "I'm sorry, I can't. I won't leave you guys."

"Smart girl," said Lucas as he motioned for her to come closer. "I have to say, I didn't think this would work." He looked over at Jessica who almost had a sad look on her face.

Gabriela nervously looked around before looking at Lucas. "Where is he?" she asked. She didn't dare mention Seth's name as her voice trembled as she tried to stay calm.

"If I'm lucky, dead!" Lucas laughed out, causing Jessica to glare at him.

"That wasn't the deal!" she yelled at him.

Lucas grabbed Gabriela and yanked her into his chest before growling at Jessica. "The deal was I collect my luna or you take her place. There was nothing mentioned about the brat! Besides, he'd only try and come back for her." He pushed past Jessica as he dragged Gabriela behind him. "Take everyone here and have them chained. They join us or they die," ordered Lucas to Diego.

Gabriela watched hopelessly as Trevor and Mara were dragged away. "Max died for doing the same thing. They will come for me and kill you too," she spat at Lucas. She glared at him as he laughed.

"If he's not dead yet, maybe he will, but when he does…he will be too late." Lucas let out a deafening howl as he headed toward the front yard of the house where red eyes seemed to emerge from all directions. "I declare this territory claimed as Red Rogue territory!" Just as the crowd began to cheer, his eyes glazed over into a dull glowing red color before going back to their original color. "Ha, it looks like your little brat of a boyfriend was captured." He turned toward Diego who had just returned. "They just linked that they will be here in ten minutes. Take them out back," he ordered Diego.

"What are you going to do?" asked Gabriela as he dragged her around the back of the house.

"You'll see." Lucas grabbed a pair of handcuffs and cuffed her hands in front of her and then pulled her into his chest. "You smell so good," he growled as she squirmed unsuccessfully to escape his grasp.

"Get off of her now!" came Seth's voice from behind. "Gabi!"

Lucas released Gabriela from his embrace and grabbed her arm with a chuckle. "And the brat has arrived! Along with his friends!" He stroked Gabriela's cheek. "I knew your dad would fall for it. I hoped my men would've killed you, but I guess it's better this way." Lucas motioned in Jessica's direction. "Jessica, grab the bag."

She glared at him as she made her way over to a large duffle bag a few yards away from where they stood. As she reached down to grab it, she looked up at Seth who was glaring daggers in her direction, but as her gaze jumped from person to person, her eyes froze as they landed upon Damien. She felt her wolf begin to stir within as he stared back at her.

"I don't have all day!" came Lucas's voice, snapping her back to reality. "I have a mate and a pack to claim, so hurry up!" he roared.

Jessica obediently made her way back next to Lucas with the bag.

"Open it and move aside," he ordered.

She bent down to unzip it but stopped. "What's in here?" she asked. When he growled at her, she stood back up and squared her shoulders. "What are you going to do?" she asked defiantly.

"Do as I say or you can learn to be useful back home," he growled in an alpha tone, causing her to whimper.

She bent down and obediently unzipped the bag but gasped at its contents. "Silver?" she choked out in fear as her eyes fell upon silver chains, cuffs, and weapons of all sorts. "What is this for?" She stood up and took a step back.

"This is to help people choose. They can join my pack or die…this is to just speed the process along." He shoved Gabriela to Diego as he pulled on a pair of thick gloves. "Bring me the other alpha first," he ordered as he pointed to Damien.

Damien struggled as two men dragged him forward and forced him to his knees in front of Lucas. "Now, surrender your pack to me…" growled Lucas.

Damien growled in return as Lucas grabbed a silver knife and slashed his arm. "Fuck you!" he spat. He pulled again against the men holding him again as Lucas slashed him again. "I will kill you!" he yelled at him before turning his attention to Jessica. "And you," he began, "you disgust me." It pained him to say those words to her but he had no choice. His hunch about her being his mate was correct, and the way she reacted when their eyes met meant that she knew they were mates, and she still obeyed Lucas. He rolled his eyes as her eyes filled with tears.

"Oh, this is wonderful!" Lucas clapped as he watched the interaction between Damien and Jessica. "You're mates! Ha! All of this to take over a pack when you were mated to an alpha?" He laughed as he motioned for Diego to bring him Gabriela. "I guess in the end, someone always loses."

Lucas smiled as he took Gabriela from Diego. "Anyone who decides not to join me, stands against me… If you stand against me, then you stand beneath me! All those who turn my offer down will be killed at sunrise, so choose wisely." He turned and winked at Seth before looking at Jessica. "Now, if you'll excuse me… I have a mate to claim."

He began to pull a struggling, screaming Gabriela toward the house. "Please," she pleaded. "Jessica, you're Damien's mate! You heard him! He's going to kill him! Don't let him do this!" she cried. "Jessica, please!"

"Shut up," growled Lucas as he tightened his grip on Gabriela's arm. "Jessica, ignore her and go help round everyone up," he ordered as he continued to walk away.

Jessica stood frozen in place as she watched Lucas drag Gabriela step-by-step to the house. She flinched at each word that came out her mouth. Gabriela was right. She betrayed her pack thinking she would be luna with Gabriela out of the picture, and nothing has gone right ever since. She turned and looked at Damien with shame in her eyes as he hung his head in defeat. She felt the tears run down her face as Lucas's men pulled Damien back toward Seth and Jace. She struggled with her thoughts and feelings, but when one of the men punched Damien in the stomach, something snapped inside her.

"No!" she growled out, causing everyone to stop and look at her. She turned toward Lucas and growled.

"What?" he asked, amused. "I'm sorry, but I thought I heard you defy your alpha."

Jessica squared her shoulders and stood tall. "You. Are. Not. My. Alpha." She took a calculated step so that she was standing next to the bag of weapons. "You are a manipulative, lying asshole!" she yelled.

She bent down and pulled out a gun and pointed it in Lucas's direction as she angled herself between where Lucas held Gabriela and his men held Jace, Seth, and Damien. Once she was a safe distance between them, she turned her gun toward Lucas's men.

"Let them go," she ordered as she clicked the safety off. "Now." The men growled as they complied and stepped away. She turned her attention back to Lucas who still held Gabriela tightly. "Her next…let her go."

"You are in no position to make demands." He extended his claws out of his hands into her arm, causing her to scream out. "I thought you were smarter than this."

Jessica glared at Lucas before looking at Gabriela, but her eyes were soft and kind. "I was right, you know." She nodded slowly at Gabriela as they locked eyes with each other. "Humans can only *cower* and *bow down* to a werewolf's presence…and *hide* from the danger."

Lucas growled before laughing out. "You defy me and still have the mind to talk down to her. You're crazier than I am." He chuckled and yanked on Gabriela's arm, who was nodding in understanding back at Jessica.

When he pulled on her arm again, Gabriela threw her head back as hard as she could into Lucas's chest and elbowed him, causing him to loosen his grip enough for her to drop to the ground. "You little bi—" he managed to say at Gabriela but stopped when a gunshot rang out.

Lucas looked down at the hole in his stomach and stumbled backward as Gabriela scooted herself backward. After it registered that he had been shot, he let out a roar and took a step forward just as Jessica fired again, sending another bullet, tearing through him just underneath his rib cage. He staggered backward and put a hand over the new bullet hole and pointed at Jessica with the other. When Jessica saw Seth rush to Gabriela's side and pull her into a hug, she felt something within her snap. Jessica took aim again at Lucas and began to fire shot after shot into Lucas as she cried freely until the gun clicked repeatedly.

"He's dead," she heard Damien say to her softly.

She kept crying as she continued to pull the trigger before dropping to her knees. She felt Damien take the gun from her hands and pulled her into his chest. "How could I have been so blind?" she cried into his chest. "I turned against my pack! My friends and family!"

"Shhh, it's over now." Damien rocked Jessica back and forth as he tried to comfort her. "He's gone."

She pulled away from Damien. "No, it's not. I did this!" She recoiled away from him as he reached for her again. "I knew it was wrong, and I did it anyway."

She watched Gabriela and Seth make their way toward her. "Nothing I say can excuse what I've done," she said to her. "Nothing I do can fix the damage that I've caused." She hung her head in shame as the words left her lips.

Gabriela shook her head. "Jessica, you're wrong." She pulled away from Seth and walked up to Jessica and pulled her into a hug. "You saved me...you saved us. All of us," she said to Jessica before pulling out of the hug. "That sounds like a pretty good start to a fix. What you did speaks louder than any apology," she said, looking into her eyes. "Right, Damien?"

Damien slowly approached the two girls. "Sounds like a pretty good start to me."

Chapter 35

"Kitten! We're going to be late! Damien and Jessica are downstairs already!"

Gabriela rolled her eyes as she grabbed her bag and dashed out the door and headed for the steps. "Seth, you were supposed to tell me when they were on their way, not when they're already here!" She ran down the stairs and ran into Jace's back.

"Gabi, you dented my back," he joked.

"Ha, ha. Very funny." She sidestepped him as he watched her drag her bag. "Where is your alpha?" she asked in a mocking tone. "He yelled for me to hurry up, and he's not here."

"Well, *my* alpha is with his luna talking to Alpha Trevor and Luna Mara, but *your* alpha said it's not his fault if you get left."

Gabriela stomped her foot as she dragged her bag the rest of the way through the house and out the door to where Seth stood with everyone else. "Seth! You repacked my bag?"

He chuckled as Gabriela glared at him. "Only a few things. Your outfits were little too…" He let his voice trail off as Gabriela put her hand on her hip.

"Too what? You took out all my sweaters and jeans. I'm not wearing the tiny outfits you put in there. Where did you find them?"

Jessica giggled as Seth shot a look in her direction. "He told Damien who told me. He swore it was for a good cause. I swear." She laughed. "At least I picked out your favorite color."

Gabriela and Jessica watched Damien and Seth pack their SUV for their summer vacation they were about to take. It had been six months since Lucas's attack. Since then, Gabriela and Seth had finally mated. Damien finally accepted Jessica as his mate after she stood trial for her crimes at both packs.

"We are going shopping when we get there. You know, I hate those tiny clothes," whined Gabriela. "They show too much skin."

"We're going to the beach. Besides, Seth said he would love to see you in that bathing suit."

Gabriela pouted playfully. She and Jessica had become surprisingly close. Seeing as how Jessica plotted her beach wear, she turned toward Seth who was joking with Damien. "So, Seth, how long are we going to be gone?"

He shrugged his shoulders before placing a kiss to her forehead. "Dad and Karina said we have the whole summer to do what we want. Dad and Trevor have some things they need to work out before we come back and start alpha training."

"Everything's about to change. Are you ready for that?" she asked.

Seth smiled, caressing Gabriela's face. "Kitten, with you by my side? I'm ready for anything."

About the Author

 Sharee Hidalgo, born in Baltimore, Maryland, currently lives in Maryland with her husband, Reinier, and her children. She loves to bake, do crafts, and hang out at car shows. She enjoys driving her husband's modified Honda Civic. She is a homeschool mom and an avid reader who enjoys writing werewolf and mafia novels during her free time. Someday, Sharee hopes to retire to Costa Rica where it's always warm with her French bulldog.

This is Sharee's first book ever published.

Enjoy!